DEAD nd DECIEVED

USA TODAY BESTSELLING AUTHOR

JENNIFER
REBECCA

Dead and Deceived

Copyright © 2019 Jennifer Rebecca

Cover Design by
Emma Hart

Formatting by Alyssa Garcia
www.uplifting-designs.com

Editing by Kayla Robichaux
For more information about Jennifer Rebecca & her books, visit:

www.jenniferrebeccaauthor.com

DEAD AND DECEIVED

You ever hear the phrase "embrace the suck"? Trent once told me it's an old Army saying that means make the best out of a bad situation, which is how I find myself clinking a metal can against jailhouse bars and wondering if Elvis Presley had to put up with scratchy wool blankets when he sang "Jailhouse Rock."

I'm accused of killing someone, but that can't be, because I was busy nursing my granny back to health.

With the Dangerous Dames scattered far and wide and Trent refusing to answer my calls, what am I to do other than shout *"Attica!"* and hope for the best? I need to find the real killer and fast.

My name is Shelby Whitmore, and before my inconvenient incarceration, I was a reporter for the *San Diego Metro News*. But now it looks like I'm going up the river for Murder One.

Too bad I didn't do it.

For my 7th grade teacher,

You probably won't read this. That's okay. This one's for me more than you. And all the other kids you discouraged. I'm okay, great even, and I hope they are too.

You see, I struggled in school. I had to learn to cope with dysgraphia and a touch of dyslexia, among other things. At the time, they were kicking my butt. But instead of encouraging me, you told my friends and my peers that I was dumb or slow.

Then one day, in front of me, you told my mom in a parent/teacher meeting that I would never amount to anything and she shouldn't bother trying to get the school to help me learn the material. You said I would never go to college, let alone finish high school, but we'll get back to that in a minute. I went home and cried. In fact, I cried almost every day that year.

My mom, my 6th, 8th, and countless other teachers throughout high school, understood my brain worked differently. They not only accepted that, but also encouraged it where you did not.

So, I just wanted to write you this love letter, to catch you up on my life. I graduated high school in 2002. And I did get into college. In fact, I was accepted to almost every university I applied to. I graduated in 2007. It took me five years, but I did it.

In 2016, just before my 33rd birthday, I published my first book. All while being a full-time wife and mother to three small children.

You were right. It was tough. So tough, in fact, I did want to give up. But my family, my friends, the teachers and professors who give the profession meaning, who love to teach and their students, never let me quit.

Through it all, my parents not only believed in me; they championed me, they encouraged me, and when I felt so worn down and discouraged that I couldn't keep going, they made me see that I not only *could,* but I *would.* So this is for them. This is for me. This is most definitely *not* for you.

And even after all that, I wish you well.

PROLOGUE

I DID NOT SEE THAT ONE COMING

"**Y**ou have the right to remain silent. Anything you say can and will be used against you in a court of law."

"What?" I gasp. I couldn't have heard Kane correctly. Kane is my friend. He's married to one of my closest girlfriends. He is Trent's partner on the force and once saw me naked and unconscious in my kitchen after Trent scared me and I ran into the glass slider before blacking out. He wouldn't be arresting me, right?

"Shelby," Kane calls out to get my attention. I must have drifted off. Clearly, I am in an alternate universe because he can't possibly be here to arrest me. "Are you listening to me?"

And I'm not listening. No, not really.

I'm so confused. One minute, I was in my condo watching *The Real Housewives of Beverly Hills*—one of my greatest guilty pleasures—and eating ice cream while looking at my secret stash of Bridal Magazines.

I know, I know. I shouldn't be buying *Brides* or *Modern Brides* or *Southern California Brides* until I have a ring on my finger, but I couldn't help myself. My mom says it's bad luck to buy the magazines before you wear a man's ring, kind of like putting the cart before the horse, but I know it's coming. Trent is going to propose and soon.

I can feel it.

Ever since we got back from Korea, where Kane and Sophie got hitched in a surprise wedding—surprise for Kane because it was spur of the moment, surprise for Sophie because Kane didn't tell her they had gotten married until the tea was spilled in the news—something has been different with Trent. He has the look of a man wanting to be tied down. He's ready and so am I.

And I know their marriage wasn't conventional, per se, but it was romantic as hell when you stop and think about it—Kane going all alpha badass caveman and tricking Sophie into marrying him so he wouldn't ever have to live without her. I think deep down, we all just want to be loved like that.

I would give anything, and I do mean *anything*, for Trent to carry me over his alpha badass shoulder to the altar, but mark my words, there will be an altar. I am not eloping. I have waited too goddamn long to find the man of my dreams. I put up with one douche canoe boyfriend after the next until the last one took the cake when he not only cheated on me, but beat the crap out of me too. As if it was my fault his cock slipped and fell into my best friend at the time. Fucker. And Trent and I have definitely had our ups and downs too. Our road to wedded bliss and a Target registry hasn't been paved with lilies but it was ours and I wouldn't want it any other way. Well . . . except for that time that he accidentally—so he says—pushed me into an open grave when I wouldn't go out with him. But in my defense, I was still feeling pretty raw from my relationship with James and I was in no way looking for a new man in my life. I was gun shy, so sue me.

But I know a proposal is coming . . . or at least I thought it was. Now, maybe I'm not so sure.

Trent and I have been in a really good place. We haven't fought at all, and I haven't wormed my way into any of his investigations in a really long time, so that should earn me perfect fiancée material points, right?

At least *I* think it does.

Not to mention, Trent and I have been banging like bunnies since we got back. We've been burning up the sheets not only late at night, but early in the morning too. And I'm not gonna lie, sometimes in the middle of the day when we meet for lunch at the Jewish delicatessen, he follows me into the ladies' room and we have a quickie on the counter. Our chemistry is hotter than ever and we can't get enough of each other. I know I will never not want Trent the way that I do.

So when a knock sounded on my front door, I answered it. I wasn't sure who was coming over, but life in the fast lane with the Dangerous Dames could mean anything. Not to mention my two favorite former hookers live around the corner in the next building over and stop on by from time to time to borrow a cup of vodka or a disguise.

What? It's not like we bake or some shit.

But when I answered the door, it wasn't Daisy and Alyssa wanting to catch up over some crappy television programming, or even my grandmother and her bestie after a night on the town in some "borrowed" wheels that they lifted off of Marla's boyfriend, Hal. It was Kane and Trent and a bunch of uniformed officers. And no one was smiling.

For a second, I hadn't seen Trent, because he was standing at the back of the pack—which was also odd, come to think of it—not front and center and I thought maybe Trent had been hurt on the job. San Diego is a great city that I love with all of my heart. I never want to live anywhere else, but it also has its share of crime, and life as a homicide detective is always dangerous. I worry for the day when I will get the phone call that something has happened to Trent on the job. And if that day ever comes it will gut me, but I have always known that it is a possibility and if I want to be with him, I need to be at peace with that.

But that is not what is happening here.

Although, I'm not quite sure of what is actually happening here. So when I look over Kane's shoulders to Trent, I see him look at me. His clover green eyes that have burned into mine while he slid deep into my body on more than one occasion burn me now—only not in a good way.

What the hell is happening here?

"Trent?" I ask him, but he doesn't answer. In fact, Trent turns and walks away. "Trent? What's going on?"

I move to follow him out the door, but Kane puts a hand up to stop me as two uniformed officers step up behind him to help intercede me. And I am not gonna lie—they strike an intimidating figure.

"Shelby, look at me," Kane says, and I jerk my gaze from Trent's retreating back to Kane's handsome face.

"What's going on?" I ask him this time.

"You have the right to remain silent. Anything you say can and will be held against you in a court of law. You have the right to an attorney. If you cannot afford one, one will be provided to you by the State," Kane says to me in a firm voice, one I have never heard from him before. He is always my friend, Kane, but I have the sinking feeling that here today, he is Detective Green as he reads me my Miranda Rights. I have never, in all the fun and mostly harmless trouble that I have cooked up in my life, have I ever had my rights read to me before. And I'm suddenly feeling a little scared. "Do you understand these rights as I have presented them to you?"

"Yes," I whisper as they turn me around and frisk me. "But I don't understand what you think I've done."

"Shelby Whitmore, you are under arrest for the murder of James Alexander," he says as the metal cuffs snick closed over my wrists.

Well, I did not see that one coming.

My name is Shelby Whitmore, and until this unfortunate incarceration, I was the columnist covering the Funerals and Obituaries section for the *San Diego Metro News,* but now it looks as if I'm going up the river for Murder One.

Too bad I didn't do it.

CHAPTER 1

MY BAD

"I will fucking cut you."

That probably wasn't what I should have said here in this crowded bar downtown, but you know, shit happens when you're drunk.

But I digress . . .

Last night
"Hey, girl," I answered after I hummed the T-Swift lyrics about Starbucks lovers when my phone rang in my desk—and by rang I mean danced around as it vibrated and played "Blank Space" by Taylor Swift inside the metal drawer where I tuck my belongings while I'm working in the office at the paper.

I was miraculously sitting at my desk in the newsroom at the San Diego Metro News, where I had been working for over a year now covering the Funerals and

Obituaries section. It was pretty cool, because I had never held a grownup job for this long before. Even my run at Home Depot didn't rival this one—and I was a kitchen and bath pro there. That's actually where I met Trent before I met him. He came in one night looking for cabinet hardware and spent the evening staring at my ass. I should have realized then that we were meant to be. It's like a damn Disney movie up in this bitch.

I was killing it at adulting and feeling pretty fantastic about it, so I brushed my shoulders off and listened to my granny rant about her oppressed life living in the retirement high rise for the fabulous and octogenarian sect. And by oppressed, I mean hell raising and free-wheeling. Granny and her best friend, Marla, cook up all kinds of trouble when they aren't selling dildos and other sexual paraphernalia out of their pocketbooks. You would think that was bad but really it was nothing compared to the other options that they had considered. Those options being Private Investigators who special-ized in medaling in all of Trent's cases or becoming a medical marijuana dispensary. Compared to those, giant rubber cocks are the strong favorite. I mean who doesn't like giant rubber dicks anyways?

"I need a damn drink!" she shouted through the phone line.

I pushed my long red hair back from my face and sighed before answering. "What's going on?"

"Your dad and uncle Sal, those ungrateful brats who ruined my hoo-ha, want to take my driver's li-cense away!" she hollered.

"But," I started, feeling really fucking surprised for . . . well, obvious reasons. "Correct me if I'm wrong here, but you don't have a driver's license."

"Of course I don't have a driver's license!" she rallied. "I haven't had a legal one since we invaded Iraq—*the first time!*"

I couldn't help it; I laughed. Granny always makes me smile. "I'll get on the horn right away with General Schwarzkopf and let him know," I told her with faux seriousness in my voice while I rolled my eyes.

"Stormin' Norman always did get my motor going," she said on a romantic sigh into the phone. Oh, gross. I don't need to know who my granny has had the hots for in her very long lifetime. She still likes to wax poetic about my dearly departed grandfather's penis and how it was the best one she ever saw. "Like that congressman with the one eye. He's a hottie if ever I saw one. That eye patch really moves me. And don't roll your eyes at me!"

I froze for a split second. How she could know I rolled my eyes is beyond me. Granny has always been all-seeing and all-knowing where her kids and grand-kids were concerned. It's freaking uncanny. Uncle Sal likes to tease her and say she's a witch.

"Jesus Christ, Granny!" I barked. "You can't just go around saying shit like that. And how did you know I rolled my eyes?"

"And why the hell not?" she asked me, and I could practically see her hand on her hip in my mind. "I have news for you, darling girl. I am eighty-two years old. If I can't say whatever the hell I want to now, then when can I?"

The correct answer is probably never, but I don't tell my granny that there are some things she should only say inside her head. It's not like she would listen to me anyways. For as long as I can remember, she's been kind of a loose cannon. Granny always says what pops into her head whether it's polite to say or not. If it's not something she should say out loud, she tries to whisper. It's just usually a very loud whisper that every in a four-mile radius can still hear. She's got a voice that really carries.

Instead, I say, "Okay."

"Okay?" she asked me.

"You're right," I agreed with her for the sake of moving on. "YOLO and all that jazz."

"YOLO!" she shouted back. Granny and Marla had adopted the You Only Live Once acronym as their life mantra. I'm still not totally convinced that it's a good thing. Granny and her best buddy Marla are more menace than Martha Stewart. "And I knew you rolled your eyes, because I see everything, my dear. I am the great and powerful Oz!"

"I believe it," I mumbled into the phone.

"So, girl's night out?" Granny circled back to what I could only assume was the purpose of her midday phone call.

"Sure!" I agreed. "Trent said he had to work late tonight, so I can come out and play."

"Excellent!" she cheered.

"Dinner too, or just drinks?" I asked wanting to know if I should grab a burger on my way home from the office. I never could hold my alcohol well and if I try to keep up with my old ladies on a empty stomach I was sure to regret it.

"We'll eat at the bar," she answered. "Get dressed

up too. I had my hair set today and I want to show it off."

I also love getting dressed up. Really, I would take any excuse to get dressed up, so I agreed readily. "Of course."

"We'll pick you up at seven," she said. "Don't be late!"

"I wouldn't dream of it," I told her before we wrapped up our call.

I had gone back to work typing up my latest obituaries for the paper, when my phone began bouncing around on top of my desk while it vibrated and played Taylor Swift's "I Knew You Were Trouble."

Speaking of vibrate, if Trent was going to have another late night burning the midnight oil, I might just have to take matters into my own hands.

Literally.

"Hello?" I answered the call after I slid my finger across the screen to unlock it.

"Hey, baby," Trent's whiskey smooth voice rumbled over the line.

"Hey, yourself." I couldn't help the flirty voice that overtook my own, nor the smile that had spread across my face. What I feel for Trent is like nothing I've ever felt before. Trent is the real deal, and so help me God, I think he feels the same way.

In fact, I think Trent might be ready to get down on one knee. And I'm not going to lie, when he does, I'll totally get down on my knees in some premarital gratitude. But not anal. My feelings on letting the old dog in the backdoor have not changed and Trent's blood engorged mayonnaise cannon isn't going master this ass anytime soon.

"I have to work late tonight," he reminded me.

"I know," I told him, wondering why he was calling. We had already talked about his late schedule this morning. "We already talked about this."

"I was hoping you'd meet me for a dinner rush quickie," he said, and I had to clench my thighs together to keep from rubbing them against each other like a cricket. Even though what he was saying to me was a little rude, it still turned me on.

What could I say? I was a sucker for Trenton Foyle and his bologna love sub.

"A booty call?" I had asked on a laugh.

"Maaaybeee," he singsonged and laughed. "So will you come down and meet me? I'll make it worth your while."

"You usually make it worth my while," I informed him.

"Usually?" he shouted through the line.

"Almost always."

"Almost!" he shouted again. "It sounds like I have to defend my honor. You better not be late."

"No can do, big man," I told him. "Tonight is ladies' night. I'm going out with the girls."

"You gonna tie one on?" Trent asked me and his voice had dropped several octaves to the sex voice.

"Most definitely," I answered nodding my head like an idiot because he obviously couldn't see me so who know why I was nodding in the first place.

"Do me a favor, baby?" he asked.

"Yeah?"

"Don't get too drunk, and I won't work too late,"

he suggested.

"And why should I not get too drunk?" I asked. "You know it's always a good time when the girls are out on the town."

"So I can fuck you while you're buzzed," Trent answered. "That will definitely make it worth your while because fucking you drunk is definitely worth *my* while."

"Yeah?" I asked. "How so?"

"Baby, you're a wildcat when you have a few drinks on deck and when you come home you can't get enough of my cock," he answered and I can hear the cocky smile in his voice.

"Trent."

"And my fingers in your pussy and my mouth. "You want me to eat you tonight?"

"Yes," I whispered.

"That's what I thought," his deep voice rumbled down the line. "Your pussy is so sweet I could eat it for hours."

"Trent—" I had started.

"Are you gonna ride my cock, go wild for my cock, and let me fuck you hard?"

"Yes."

"Are you wet right now?" he asked. "Tell me, baby."

"Yes," I whispered squirming in my crooked office chair.

"Have a good time tonight, baby," he said. "But don't get too drunk so I can fuck my wildcat. I really like to fuck my wildcat."

"Deal."

And with that, Trent hung up and I was left more than a little hot and bothered.

I worked the rest of the day before heading to my condo to shower and style my red hair as girls-night-out sexy as I could. I did a smoky eye look and a shimmery nude lip before spritzing a little perfume on my neck. Usually, I wore that sweet one Julia Roberts advertised on TV, but tonight I went with something smoky and a little spicy. I can't help but let my mind wander over all of the things Trent had previously mentioned.

I padded naked to my closet, pulled on a black lace strapless bra and matching cheeky panties, because Trent really liked my ass, and I liked to watch him come a little unglued when he saw it packaged so nicely. I pulled my dark jeggings up my legs then slipped a black silk camisole top with lace trim from its hanger and dropped it on over my head.

I stepped into my favorite black patent leather pumps then headed down the hall to the kitchen. Missy jumped up on the counter and let out a complaint for wet food with a harsh, "Meow!"

"Who's my gorgeous girl?" I cooed, scratching her under the chin before popping open a can of wet cat food, which smelled like rotting fish in hell. But by the happy swish of her tail, she was totally into it, so I spooned out a big glob into her food bowl.

I had just dumped my wallet, phone, and lipstick into my black clutch when the doorbell rang. "Don't wait up, Miss!" I called as I headed for the front door.

"Woo, girl. Lookin' good!" Daisy snapped her fingers back and forth in front of me after I opened the door.

"Thanks," I said back on a smile. "You too."

Daisy, my retired hooker bestie, was in a poison-green—her signature color—tube top and dark wash skinny jeans with matching green heels and hoop earrings. For her, it was a pretty sedate outfit. And as always, she rocked it. Daisy was one of those women who radiate confidence and it was an attractive quality. I had met Daisy in jail a little over a year ago when Trent had locked me up in a misguided attempt to protect me. Daisy had been picked up for selling her wares of the flesh to those with deep pockets and some interesting sexual appetites. Somewhere between then and now, we have become inseparable. I'm not sure I could live without her. She is by far, one of the best friends I have ever had.

I admired her and all that she was. Daisy, and now Sophie and Alyssa, were the first friends I had in a long time. And I was glad to have them.

I was a lone wolf.

It's not that I never had friends before. I had a close group of girlfriends all through college. My best friend Bella and I were so similar. We liked all the same things and we called ourselves platonic soulmates. We took all the same classes in school and we belonged to the same sorority. We were even roommates. Bella and I did everything together.

Apparently, we also both banged my fiancé, James. That was unfortunate.

One night, after a long day of working at Home Depot in the kitchen and bath department, I had come home to find Bella bent over the arm of our sofa.

"Oh," I'd said. "I'm sorry."

I had started to back out of our apartment until I realized it was my fiancé who was plowing her from behind.

I had run out of the apartment and just drove around. I had nowhere to go. I had no one. My dad had just retired from the Army and my parents were celebrating on a yearlong cruise around the world. I was watching their house and their plants and my grandparents.

When I realized my childhood home in Rancho Penasquitos was empty and the perfect place for me to lick my wounds, I had raced on over.

I should have checked into a hotel.

In fact, later, I would have wished I had. But what followed changed the course of my life forever. I probably could have forgiven the affair. Looking back, I was an idiot. I know I would have forgiven them both and gone on with my life as if nothing had happened. Hell, Bella was going to be my Maid of Honor. What a joke!

But when James found me holed up at my mom and dad's house later that night, he was furious—with me! And that made me so angry I practically had steam pouring out of my ears. The Whitmore temper is legendary. My dad, my granny, and my grandfather can all go from zero to fifty in the blink of an eye. And I'm no exception to the rule.

"It's over!" I shouted. "Get out!"

"You are not the boss here," James seethed as he prowled closer to me. "Now here's how it's going to go. You are going to get your shit and go home. And it is not your business who I fuck."

"No."

"I did not ask for your opinion, Shelby," he snapped. "You are going to go on as if nothing happened. I deserve a wife who comports herself appropriately. So show me that you deserve the role over Bella."

"No," I had said before my brain could catch up to how angry he really was. "I'm taking myself out of the running."

When he struck me, I hadn't seen it coming. The stars that had danced in front of my eyes had caught me off guard. The next blow took me to my knees.

"Some lessons need to be learned the hard way."

I had closed my eyes against his onslaught until finally I let go and fell into the darkness of nothing. The darkness didn't find me lacking. The darkness didn't cheat on me. The darkness didn't hurt, so I had welcomed it with open arms.

When the darkness spit me back out into the world and I opened my eyes, everything hurt. My entire body had felt broken and bruised, and I tasted the coppery tang of blood in my mouth.

I tried to push myself up to stand, but my legs buckled underneath me. I crawled on my belly using my arms to pull me toward the table next to the sofa that had a landline on it. It was slow going, but I made it there.

My parents had never not had a landline and swear they will never live without one, because they are so much safer. Right then, I was just glad there was a phone nearby, because I needed help and I knew I wouldn't make it far in my battered state.

I knew I wouldn't make it up the sofa, so I reached for the cord to the phone and yanked it toward me as soon as I wrapped my fingers around it. They slipped several times before I could get a fair purchase. Blood slicked my hands, keeping me from getting a good hold.

When the phone finally fell to the floor, the receiver tumbled off of the base and the dial tone sounded throughout the room. I quickly looked around to make sure James wasn't still there. I didn't want to get caught seeking help, even though I was sure I would die without it.

I picked up the receiver and my fingers tripped over the number I had known by heart since I was six years old.

"Hello?" my grandfather answered after the first ring. That's something that always made me laugh. They never let the phone go unanswered. They never let it go to the answering machine.

"PopPop," I whispered. "I need help."

"Where are you?" he demanded.

"I'm at Mom and Dad's house."

After my grandfather hung up, he raced down the road to my parents' place. They didn't live very far from each other at the time. When he found me, he cursed up a blue streak and then called an ambulance.

My grandfather was always the one I could turn to for anything, so when he begged me to tell him who hurt me, I caved even though I tried not to. I just wanted to move on. When I told him what had happened with James and Bella that night, he said I would never see them again, and by then I agreed with him. After James beat the snot out of me, I could see the writings on the wall. There would be no forgiving and forgetting.

And when James had shown up at the hospital looking for me, my grandfather lost it.

"You son of a bitch!" my grandfather roared before he punched James in the face, a total K.O. James folded like a lawn chair, and I'm not gonna lie—it brought me a little bit of joy after the pain he caused me, both emotional and physical.

But then my grandfather had clutched his chest and collapsed. He'd had a massive heart attack. The hospital staff said he was dead before he hit the ground.

I was wrong when I'd thought I would die that night. It was my grandfather who wouldn't walk away, and I would forever blame myself.

Shortly after his death, Granny had packed up her life and moved into the Peaceful Sunset Retirement Complex downtown. I moved into their condo. And I adopted a cat. Who needs men or friends when you have a cat? I was totally down to embark on my life as a crazy cat lady.

For months afterward, every time I ran into Bella around town, she would throw it in my face that I couldn't keep James happy. She loved telling me how I was never good enough.

Needless to say, it made trusting people difficult at best. I had my granny, and she was all I needed. That was, until she and her friends pulled me into their group and refused to let me go. When I met Daisy in jail over a year ago, she announced that we were going to be best friends, and so far she's held up her end of the bargain tenfold.

Sophia and Alyssa fell into our group as well, and

now I couldn't imagine a time in my life without any of them.

"Let's get a move on chick!" Daisy called out as she smacked my ass, which jiggled a little bit in my tight jeans, bringing me out of the memory.

I laughed as I locked the front door behind us and followed her down the walkway to the parking lot, where Granny and Marla were waiting in the front seats of Hal's vintage powder blue Caddy. When she saw us, Granny hopped out and folded back the seat so Daisy and I could climb in. Alyssa was already in the back seat, which was crowded with all our asses crammed across the bench seat.

"Hit it!" Marla crowed from the front passenger seat once we were all safely sealed inside the car—and safe was a term I used loosely when my grandmother's driving was concerned. I made a mental note to talk to my mom about Granny's driving without a license. I couldn't tell Trent, because he frowned on the slightly-less-than-legal activities of either myself or our grand-mothers. Sometimes is was easier to ask for forgive-ness than beg for permission and I was not raised to beg for anything.

Granny pressed the accelerator and headed for the Belly Flop, a favorite dive bar in Mission Bay. I know I shouldn't be taking the grannies to a dive bar, but I figured it was better that I'm with them than not. And the truth was, they were a hoot!

As Granny took the turn into the parking lot on two wheels, the tires screeched as she slammed on the brakes and narrowly avoided hitting the side of an old brick building with the numbers 1801 down the side. I jumped out of the car with sweaty palms and no idea that tonight my life would change forever.

"Let's get our drank on!" Granny shouted like the rapper she is deep down in her soul as we walked in the door. Sometimes when I look at her, I think she would be a great third wheel to the Martha Stewart and Snoop Dog duo.

My posse and I walked in like Charlie's Angels with the wind blowing our hair. Granny even tried her best at an over-the-shoulder hair flip, although to my knowledge she's had her hair trimmed short and set every week since the early 1980s. Still, the effect was there for sure.

We ponied up to the bar like we owned the place. We were like lady gunslingers in an old western movie. Like lade desperados with the world bowing at our patent leather and compression stocking feet.

Maybe.

Okay, probably not.

"What'll it be, ladies?" the bartender asked when he got down to our end of the bar. He's cute as in really cute. He has his head shaved bald and while that doesn't usually do it for me, he looks great. He also sports an awesome beard and as he talks, a silver barbell winks at me from inside his mouth. I have always heard that a tongue piercing can be an interesting thing but this guy and his are not for me.

"Vodka and cranberry, please," Alyssa ordered politely.

"Tequila," Daisy's voice boomed through the bar.

"Make that two," Granny said.

"Make it three," I added. I loved tequila, even though I knew I shouldn't. It was the first drink to mess me up in college, so I knew I should stay away. Granted, Bella and I were dumb and underage and mixed it with vodka—a killer combination for sure.

"Diet Coke for me," Marla said. "I'm the driver."

The bartender didn't say anything after we told him what we wanted, but he did make the sign of the cross like a good Catholic boy when Marla announced she was our designated driver for the evening, so there was that. I bit down on my bottom lip to keep from laughing. I mean, he wasn't wrong, but we survived this far with her on the road; what was one more night?

He slapped drink after drink on the bar top in front of us, and when he set the last one down, Granny raised her glass signaling a toast "to all the single ladies" as she put it. We all raised our glasses up high and waited for her to impart her lifelong wisdom on us.

And let me tell you, my granny does not disappoint.

"Ladies," she started. "May your pussies always be wet and the dicks always be hard!" And then she throws back her tequila to the tune of Marla's cackles.

"Jesus," I shuddered before throwing back my shot.

"Oh, man," Marla barely got out through her hilarity. "You should see your faces. That was a good one, Verna."

"Good man!" I called to the bartender. I was definitely starting to feel the surplus of alcohol and lack of food.

"Yeah?" he said when he sauntered back down the bar.

"I'm going to need the bottle."

"Coming right up," he said on a chuckle before grabbing the bottle and pouring me another shot.

"So, speaking of hard dicks..." Granny led off, and the bartender, who was kind of hot not that I looked at him over much, but not as hot as Trent, froze as Granny spoke. The shot glass he was filling up overflowed as the liquor kept pouring out of the bottle suspended in his hand.

"Hey, man!" I snapped my fingers in front of his face. "Don't waste the good tequila." I had no idea how those words sound outside of my head, because at that point, I was two tequila shots deep, and while I loved tequila, tequila did not love me back. Whatever it was, it seemed to work, because he jumped, putting the bottle upright.

"Oh shit!" he said as he grabbed a rag from below the bar and started mopping up the tequila mess.

I simply threw my next shot back and let my buzz mellow for a bit. I could've also maybe gone for some nachos. They were like the tacos of drunk food. I should've probably put some food in my belly to absorb some of the alcohol, or it was going to be a night a puking before Trent ever showed and we got to the drunk sexing.

"Can I get you ladies anything else?" the cute bartender asked.

"Yeah," I piped up. "Can I have some nachos please?"

"For you, sugar, anything," he said on a wink before heading off to put my order in with the bar and leaving me with the feeling that if I had ordered him he would have been okay with it. The feeling was weird.

It has been a long time since I had anyone flirt with me. I just let the moment drift into the ether because I'm not about to get tangled up with anyone that isn't Trent. He's it for me.

"Now that there," Granny said as she tipped her glass toward where the bartender disappeared, "has trouble written all over him."

"I have no idea what you're talking about," I said, more than a little put out by the idea that my own granny would think I would consider stepping out on Trent. "I wouldn't go there even if I wanted to, and I most definitely don't want to."

"Good," was all she left it at. And no other comment was needed. Granny had made her point and like the southern lady she was, she could score her point and walk away without rubbing it in my face.

While we'd had our ups and downs, I wouldn't throw that all away for a night of what promised to be mediocre sex and a little attention thrown my way. Sure, Trent had been working a lot since we all got back from Korea a few weeks ago. But so had Kane. They caught a homicide case almost as soon as the wheels of our airplane touched down at Lindbergh Field, and it had been one right after another ever since. That was the life of a homicide detective and his main squeeze— or in Sophie's case, his wife.

Honestly, I was a little jealous that Kane went all caveman in Korea and tricked Sophie into marrying him. That was kind of hot. But I would bide my time and wait for Trent to make an honest woman out of me. What I was not going to do was settle for a little flirtation from a bartender in my favorite dive bar during this busy murder season.

"So where is Sophie tonight?" I asked the crowd. "Has anyone heard from her in a while?"

"She's good," Alyssa answered. Sometime between Korea and now, they'd become close, and I made a mental note to have coffee with her this week. "She said she was feeling a little under the weather and just wanted to crash with a book before she had to get up early to train the team of tiny demons."

"They're not demons," Granny said on a laugh. "Those are just a bunch of normal six-year-olds."

"Yikes," I mumbled to myself as Alyssa gave in to a shudder that rolled down her spine. Looked like neither of us were in the market for kids anytime soon.

"Here you go," he said as he placed a platter heavy with chips and cheese and all the toppings in front of us, plus a stack of appetizer plates that none of us were going to use. We were all just going to stuff our gobs while we drank until it was time to call it a night. I had no idea when that would be, so I just pulled a chip from the stack and made sure it was loaded up before I stuffed it in my face.

I had just thrown back another shot of tequila before shoving another fully loaded chip in my mouth when I heard a voice from over my shoulder that I really wished I hadn't. It had been about six months since the last time James Alexander darkened my door and I had really hoped that I had heard the last of him. Unfortunately, at that time, he was there to kidnap me. Daisy and I were hot on the trail of a serial killer who was murdering her fellow ladies of the night when James nabbed me from George Washington's Strip Club and chained me to a bathroom sink in a seedy motel this side of Mexico. He had said I needed to come to my senses and marry him even though I was clearly dating a police officer—and he should know because James had admitted to stalking me for a while before that moment in the motel that I will never forget.

Trent rescued me, and James had been in the wind ever since. Although, I had to admit, I didn't follow up on him like I should have. I was pretty sure there was something said at the time about filing charges and paperwork and . . . well . . . I'm not really one for paperwork, so I could almost guarantee it didn't actually happen.

My bad.

So when I heard that gratingly patronizing voice, I immediately regretted my lack of follow through. When I turned around, I saw he was even closer to me than I realized, and I'm not gonna lie—a Temporary Restraining Order would've been a pretty great thing right about then. I'm sure he used his fancy money connections and sweet talked his way out of the charges while I wasn't paying attention. And that's kind of on me. I should have filed the paperwork.

Fucking paperwork.

"Nice mustache," James snickered as he waved a condescending finger around the vicinity of my mouth. For a split second, I felt like the insecure college coed that I was when we were together and patted my mouth to find a glob of sour cream smeared across the corner of my mouth.

"What are you doing here?" I asked.

"I'm going to get you back," he answered, as if it

was obvious and I was a complete and total idiot.

"Dude, you kidnapped me," I responded, feeling my face flush red as my temper flared. "And I'm still pissed about that."

"That mouth will only get you into even more trouble one day, but I have something else to occupy it," he evaded my question and rolled his eyes.

"A Vienna sausage would occupy more," Granny snarked from her place behind me over at the bar.

"Come back to me," James pleaded, and for a split second I saw a flash of that charismatic man that I had fallen in love with years ago.

And then it was gone and I saw the jerk who lurked under the flashy surface.

"I'm with Trent now, and you're with Bella," I reminded him in a calm and quiet voice.

"Not any more I'm not," James contradicted.

I didn't really know what to say to that. Bella and James were a sure thing. Especially after they banged like bunnies behind my back for years. I didn't know Bella was plotting to usurp my life in a hostile takeover in her own version of "Single White Female." I was really upset for about two-point-five seconds, but then James showed up and beat the crap out of me. And when I woke up in the hospital, I was pretty glad I'd just dodged a bullet—that is until I realized I'd inadvertently caused my grandfather's death.

It took a long time for me to come to terms with the fact that I didn't cause his heart attack but a deranged man from his old unit in Vietnam had been switching out his heart medications and leaving him unprotected. When the stress of rescuing me finally took its toll, his heart had just stopped.

"Also, I want my bowie knife back," James demanded.

"You'll get it when I stab you in your cold, dead heart." Okay, for real, maybe I should've laid off the tequila. That was just a wee bit aggressive. Don't get me wrong; I hate him more than just about anyone in this world, but still, even I'm not homicidal.

And trust me, I would know. I have met many a psychotic killer in the last two years.

"Dude!" someone shouted from somewhere in the bar. I don't really have time to pay attention to everyone else in this establishment. When James is around I need to be completely focused on him and his dirty deeds or else he will get the drop on me and I swore while I was handcuffed to that bathroom sink that it would be the last time James ever hurt me again. "Someone call the cops."

"We shall see," James said in an arrogant way that was not at all sexy like it was when Trent is more than a little cocky. Speaking of Trent, James was totally killing my buzz that was going to lead to adventurous drunk sex, and I really, really was looking forward to adventurous drunk sex.

"We won't see anything," I replied on a frustrated sigh. Somehow, with James, I was always left feeling more than a little frustrated.

"Sure." He rolled his eyes in his way that told me what a moron he thought I was and how much it tried his patience. I really fucking hated that eye roll about as much as I really fucking hated how he completely disregarded my feelings and wishes. As if I would just cave to whatever it was that he wanted.

"I will fucking cut you." That probably wasn't what I should have said there in that crowded bar downtown, but you know, shit happens when you're drunk.

"Someone should really call the police," I heard someone say from somewhere in the bar as I leaned into him to poke him in the chest to emphasis my point.

"You always were such a cunt."

"Thanksss," I snarked as I held out the S at the end, making the word hiss like a snake as it left my mouth.

"This isn't the last of this," he threatened.

I leapt toward him. I just wanted to punch his stupid, smarmy face in. Just a little bit. But Daisy and Alyssa must have seen the angry look of intent on my face, because they plucked me out of the air midleap, like it was all part of a choreographed dance, kind of like the big leap and lift at the end of "Dirty Dancing." I always did love that movie. Then they tackled me to the sticky floor of the bar.

And then James rolled his eyes again, turned on his heel, and walked out of the bar as if he hadn't a care in the world.

"That went dark, girl," Daisy said from her spot on top of me in the dog pile.

I responded the only way I could. "My bad."

And then the cops showed up.

CHAPTER 2

CHECK, PLEASE

Last night

"**D**o you want me to look in your eyes while I blow you?" I asked as I batted my eyes innocently at the officer that responded to whatever call went out about the fight James and I had in the bar.

"Babe," Trent said from his place next to the uniformed officer. I could hear the mix of his amused laughter with his frustration at his plans for the night being waylaid in his voice as he rolls his eyes at me but in a nice way. I know that sounds weird—and it may have been the tequila talking here—but Trent rolled his eyes at me in a loving way. Somewhere around me, I heard Granny snicker as only she could when she found something that was usually wildly inappropriate and funny. It just so happened that it was also usually hilarious, just as it was also usually something monumentally stupid that I said or did.

"What?" I asked with faux innocence. I know that

I was behaving badly but I don't care. This kind of delicious yet harmless mischief is so fun to cook up. I love it.

"Seriously, Shelby?" He smirked. And freaking love that smirk. There is something about the look that shows his confidence in a sexy way not an arrogant one. The way it plays around his mouth and his dark stubble across his cheeks. I love all of it. I love this man.

"Do I need to breathalyzer her, sir?" the officer asked Trent and he looked so nervous it's adorable. The officer is definitely younger than me and I'm only twenty-five. He's probably straight out of the academy and looked terrified as he looked at Trent unsure of what to do. Trent looked like her didn't know whether to laugh or to punch the young officer in the face for having impure thoughts about me.

But the look he gave me said I was absolutely going to get my ass paddled for putting us all in this situation. I squeezed my thighs together to ease some of the burn between them but it was no use. I couldn't wait.

"What?" I asked as if I was posing the most important question in the history of the universe. "It was an honest question."

"No," he replied on a chuckle while giving me a highly indecent side-eye. "You don't need to breathalyzer her. She isn't driving, and I doubt the bartender is going to press charges."

"I didn't see anything," the cute bartender said as if on cue.

Smart man.

I should have learned from him and kept my mouth

shut.

Too bad I would find out much, much later that it was already too late. The wheels of fate were in motion.

Run!

So it was a hot minute—or at least that's what it felt like in my drunk girl brain—after that slimy, limp-dicked, little weasel slid out of the bar like a shart in a pair of dingy tightie-whities before the 5-0 rolled in. The blue-and-red lights of San Diego's finest swirled against the glass front of the Belly Flop.

It might've been wrong, but my first thought when I saw that the cops were there was to run. It's not that I had a fear of the police—in fact, far from it with my relationship with Trent hot and heavy as usual—or that I particularly live a life of crime. That was, unless you counted six months ago, when I posed as a hooker. But I wasn't actually hooking, I swear! I was working an undercover investigation with Daisy, my elderly grandmother, and her best friend. Granted, I wasn't working officially for any branch of law enforcement—or at all, in any capacity, if I was being honest.

But Trent and I were finally in a really good place, and I would hate to rock the boat. Not to mention, the whole of San Diego PD seemed to be hot under the collar to rat me out to my one and only. Those rat bastards thought it was so funny to radio my man and tell him where they found me or what I had been doing at the time. I even heard a rumor that I have my own radio code and I'm not going to lie that is kind of unflattering. So I had to keep my day-to-day on the DL.

So I was already coming up with my alibi—cough, cough, I mean *backstory*—when a certain sexy detective with dark hair and a big dick that can make me see stars sauntered in like he owned the place. I picked up my glass and threw back a mouthful of tequila in a manner befitting a bearded gunslinger in an old western movie and gasped as the liquor burned my lungs. I slammed the glass onto the bar top with more force than I originally intended, and I winced when it landed with a heavy thud on the scarred wood. I am more than a little surprised the glasses didn't so much as crack. It hit that hard.

My bad.

And then, after having spent my evening behaving like a sailor on liberty after being away at sea for years and landed in the middle of fleet week, I waited for the previously mentioned sex god in the body of a homicide detective to make his way to me.

Later, I would make sure he made me come so many times during some adventurous drunk sex. That was, if it was still on the table. By the cocky grin on his face, I would say it's still on the table. Woohoo!

"Babe," Trent said on a low chuckle. "'Adventurous drunk sex'?"

"I said that out loud, didn't I?" I asked while I worried my bottom lip between my teeth. I always do that when I'm nervous or a little embarrassed. I'll admit that I don't embarrass easily so that is a rare occurrence, but I do worry often. Especially where Trent is concerned. He just makes me feel so off kilter. But usually only in a good way. Usually.

"Oh yeah," he answered, and I began to fret that maybe he possibly could have definitely maybe heard the rest of it. That is unfortunate.

"Did . . . umm . . . did you maybe hear anything else I shouldn't have said out loud?" I asked, and Trent's smirk spread into a full-on smile that made the lines beside his eyes crinkle in a delicious way. It almost distracted me, but I knew better. This wasn't my first rodeo. I had been down this road before.

I was fucked.

"You mean the part about me being a sex god with a giant, magical penis in my pants?"

As soon as the words left his stupid, handsome mouth, I instantly wished the ground would open up and swallow me whole. If I don't drop dead of mortification right here and right now, I vow to devote my lie to science and find a black hole that can suck me in in times such as this one.

"Nope," he said. "I can't make that happen either. Plus, if the ground swallowed you whole, we couldn't go home and have, as you so eloquently put it, 'adventurous drunk sex.' And you seem to like my huge dick a whole lot, so—"

I slapped my hand over his mouth to stop his very loud speech about how much I enjoyed his penis. His breath puffs out against my head as he laughs through my fingers. This is not funny!

"Nope," I said, shaking my head. "Not today, bucko."

"So you don't want to have 'adventurous drunk sex' with me?" he asks and by his tone of voice we both know that he has me cornered and we both know it. The big, sexy jerk.

"I'm not speaking to you about this," I responded. But knowing Trent the way that I do, he is going to push the envelope. He loves to push me. Let's just hope it's not into an open grave this time.

"How about someone tell me about the argument that occurred here this evening?" the officer waded in. In the heat of the moment and all of our sexual tension snapping and sparking around Trent and I like it always does, I got more than a little turned on and I had totally forgotten about him. Whoops.

"Alleged argument," I amended his question in a haughty tone of voice. I might be drunk and a skunk and fighting a wicked snail trail here but I am not going to be dumb enough to incriminate myself in front of a police officer.

"Perhaps we need a breathalyzer reading after all," he said as he held up the small black device in front of my mouth. My eyes go wide in response and I stand the in stunned silence.

And everything kind of devolved from there.

"I don't need you to defend me," I huffed feeling more than a little annoyed over the whole situation. "I didn't do anything wrong."

"Seriously, babe?" Trent asked as if I lost my damn mind, and truth be told, I might have. I'd know for sure when the fog of tequila and bad bar food cleared but until then only time will tell. "The only reason I don't tan your ass right now is because I'm looking forward to fucking Drunk Shelby later."

His low, growled promises in that deep voice of his made me squeeze my thighs together, and by the sexy smirk on his face, he knew what he was doing to me. Although, one could argue that by the three orgasms he gave me last night and the two in the shower this morning, Trent definitely knew what he could do to me and, come to think of it, I had absolutely no complaints about it, unless it didn't involve a little P in the V in the next thirty minutes. Then I would have some complaints. I hope our plans are still ago.

"Yeah?" I asked. "I had almost completely forgotten about our tentative plans for adventurous drunk sex."

"Those plans weren't tentative," he said and I realize that Trent sees the play of my emotions across my face. Because that's not at all embarrassing.

"Whoops," I say absentmindedly. "I must have said that out loud."

"Oh yeah," Trent answered like we were the only people in this bar and not surrounded by a bunch of our closest family members and friends, not to mention a few colleagues. "Drunk Shelby is a wild cat."

"Meow," I whisper. I can't help myself. The minute Trent's sexy voice rumbles down my spine and I am lost to him. The flirty reply just slipped right out of my mouth. Lucky for me, Trent seems to like it.

"Check, please," Trent said as he snapped his fingers.

Too bad that, much later, I would wish I would have drank less and paid way more attention, but by then it would be way too late.

CHAPTER 3

ADVENTUROUS DRUNK SEX

Last night

"**W**hat do you want, baby?"

"Umm . . ." I answered. Trent and I have been together for a while now and he has seen every inch of me in a variety of compromising situations but still I struggle to give him the dirty words that he so loves to hear. Who knew that I could be shy?

"Tell me, and you can have whatever you want," Trent whispered to me as I pulled my top over my head. "All you have to do is give me the words and I'll give you your fantasies."

"Trent . . ." I pleaded, but I don't know what for. For mercy? For an orgasm or two or three? I had no clue, as I unbuttoned my jeans and pushed the material to the floor before stepping out of them and kicking them aside. All I know is that I need him. I need Trent like I have never needed anyone before.

"Give me the words, Shelby," Trent growls and

I'm helpless to do anything but exactly what he wants.

"I want to sit on your face, and then I want to sit on your cock," I whispered, feeling a blush heat my cheeks. I am more than a little shocked that, once again, Trent managed to push me past all my boundaries. At this point in our relationship, I shouldn't be surprised. We both know that he's going to push and unless it's a big deal, I'm going to cave—especially in the bedroom where it's so much fun to give in—otherwise, I'm too independent.

"Your wish is my command," he said before he crashed his mouth down on mine.

I let out a moan as I opened underneath him, tasting him as he licked into my mouth, and heat burned through my body. I broke our mouths apart and sucked in a breath as I dragged his T-shirt up over his head and threw it to the floor while his own hands battled his belt buckle. The telltale clank sounded as it hit the ground with his jeans as they hit the carpet, and he kicked them aside. His hard length sprang free and pressed against my waist. It seemed my man went without undies today.

And fuck me if that wasn't sexy.

It did something to me that heightened the happy, fuzzy feeling in my brain. I didn't need the alcohol to make me feel this way, this is all Trent and I can't live without him. He is the water that I need to survive.

He pressed his mouth behind my ear and gently kissed a path down the side of my neck as he unhooked my bra behind my back and flung it away. Trent cupped my heavy breasts in each hand and raised one to meet his mouth just before he pulled the hard tip into his mouth.

He let out a groan around my flesh that sent a shiver up my spine before he dropped down to his knees. Trent tucked his fingers into the lace waistband of my panties before sliding them down my legs. I widened my stance as he slid a finger through the wetness between my legs before burying his face between my legs. He wrapped his fist around his cock as he placed a kiss at the apex of my thighs.

"Trent," I whispered.

And then he gracefully rolled to his back with his feet hip-width apart and held out a hand to me. "Come here, Shelby."

And I did. I reached out and took his hand to let him guide me, ever so slowly, with my knees just above his shoulders. Trent dropped my hand and grabbed my hips to pull me down. He gave my center a hard lick, and I let my head tip back on my shoulders. My long, red hair fell to brush along his abs, and his fingertips pressed into my flesh on contact.

His tongue speared my center, and I let out a moan as he penetrated me over and over. I dug the pads of my fingers into his chest behind me as I leaned back, angling my hips against his mouth and I can't help but rock my hips against him.

I let his rumbling groan wash over me as it rolls through my body; I'm helpless to his call to me. Like a storm over the sea that pushes the waves over a rocky cliff, I was lost to Trent. He rolled my clit into his mouth as he mercilessly flicked his tongue over my sensitive peak, and my breath caught in my throat as wave after wave of my climax rolled over me. It was so strong and consuming in its intensity that I would be happy with just this.

But tonight, we were far from done.

I took a moment to catch my breath before climbing back down Trent's ridiculously sexy body. I knew I said I wanted to sit on his face and then ride his dick, and I still did, but we would get to that in good time. Now was when I returned the favor, at least a little bit, for his fantastic mouth.

"Shelby," he said when I settled between his thick legs. I could hear the amusement in his voice as I wrapped my fingers around his hard length and stroked him once . . . twice . . . before tucking a chunk of my hair behind my ear as I leaned forward to take the tip of him in my mouth. "What are you doing?"

"Isn't it obvious?" I asked cheekily after letting the tip of him go with a pop. I swirl the tip of him around and around in my mouth and smile when I hear his answering groan.

"I thought you were going to ride my cock?" he asked as I licked up the length of him like a lollipop before swirling my tongue around his tip again.

"Oh, I am," I informed him with a slight pause in my task at hand. "I'm just giving a little of what I got back."

Trent groaned and arched his hips toward me as I slowly took him all the way to the back of my throat. I pulled back, letting him slip almost all the way out of my mouth, before swirling my tongue around the tip and then sliding back down again, only to repeat the process again and again.

Trent threaded his finger in my hair and pulled—

almost to the point of pain, but not quite—as I sucked him deep into my mouth. I can tell that he wants me to move faster and put him out of his misery and I have absolutely no intention of doing that. *Yet.*

"Shelby—" he pleads and I smile to myself as I pretend that I don't hear him and lick around him again and again.

I slid his hard length in and out of my mouth, moving a bit faster now. I heard his gasp, and I fucking loved it. I loved bringing Trent to the edge. I want to watch him fall apart for me. I can ride his cock another time and knowing Trent the way that I do, it will be sooner rather than later.

"Baby," he said but I didn't let up.

"Un-uh," I murmured around his cock as I slide up and down his hard length.

"Shelby," he growled, just before he let go of my hair and grabbed me under my arms. He hauled me up his body as he knifed up to a sitting position and dropped me down to straddle his hips.

I felt his cock against my center as he wrapped his hand around the back of my neck, crushing his mouth to mine. As his tongue tangled with mine, I tasted the tang of myself. I rocked back and forth, letting his cock slide against me for a moment, making us both burn a little hotter as we walk the knife's edge.

I braced my hands against his chest and rose up. I felt Trent at my center and slowly slid down. I placed my feet flat against the floor and rocked my hips against his as he wrapped his arms around me and held me tight. I feel him deep and I'm lost in the moment.

"Yes," I pant as I move faster and faster, and he dug

the pads of his fingers into my hips so hard that I know it will leave marks on my skin and I love that too.

I felt my climax building higher and higher as Trent pumped his hips up into me from underneath, meeting me stroke for stroke. I have to hold on tight to his body, my fingers digging into his abs. The buzz of the tequila still swirled in my head as I rode Trent, and I felt like I was floating on a cloud made of orgasms.

That's totally a thing.

I couldn't take it anymore. My climax built so strong that I had to drop down to drape myself across Trent's strong chest. I pressed my hands on either side of his face and put my mouth to his, not so much in a kiss, but just to breathe him in and I tangle my finger into his hair to hold him close to me.

He slid his hands down to my thighs and pulled them wider so he could power up into me harder and faster than before. I gave myself over to his punishing rhythm as the tips of my toes scrape on the floor.

What was once my show to control was now Trent's, and I wouldn't have it any other way. The feeling I get when I finally give into him is indescribable. It gives me a heady rush.

And then it rolled over me. I never had a chance. The orgasm he gave me earlier was nothing in comparison, and I threw my head back and cried out as I came. Trent held me tight to his body as he plunged deep once . . . twice . . . three times more before he called out my name and followed me over the edge.

He tucked my face into the crook of his neck as our hearts still raced, the only sound in the dimly lit living room until I pushed up ever so slight to look my handsome man in his face. He smiled gently at me and my heart skipped a beat. I wasn't sure I could ever get tired of looking at Trent.

Here's hoping I have a lifetime left to do it because I never want to try to go without again.

"Adventurous enough for you?" I asked saucily. I can't help the cheeky grin that steals over my face.

"There's my wildcat," he returned, his smile widening and his eyes full of feeling. Seeing the way that I feel about Trent reflected in his eyes for me is overwhelming. I love this man so very much. "How are you feeling?"

"Still a little buzzed," I answered. "Why?"

"Because now I'm gonna fuck you slow in a bed," he growls.

"Okay," I whispered, making his smile widen.

And then Trent scooped me up and carried me into my little bedroom in the back of my condo. He laid me down on the bed with all of its throw pillows and fluffy white blankets, and he kept his promise to fuck me slow. He held me in his arms while I drifted off into a deep, peaceful sleep with a smile on my face, because I was happy—not just in this moment, but happy in my life with Trent.

Too bad tomorrow everything would change.

CHAPTER 4

DONGS FOR DAYS

"Holy Cock-a-doodle-doo, Batman," I say, more than a little stunned when Granny ushers me into her apartment that has been completely transformed. This is not what I expected. Not at all.

"I know!" she says excitedly. "Awesome, right?"

"So... *uhh*... awesome."

Earlier today

"Sweet but Psycho" by Ava Max blasted from my phone, and Trent was a dead man. All of the tequila I drank the night before pounded through my skull, and for a nerve-wracking minute, I wasn't so sure it wouldn't make a reappearance.

Trent thought he was so funny. Every time it came on the radio, he said, "Oh, it's your song, babe." He particularly liked the part about a hot ass but she's still psycho. A glowing reference, I'm sure. Trent just laughs like it's so adorable that I'm kind of crazy.

Well, har-dee-har-har.

I would murder him for it but he also likes to tell me that he thinks my particular brand of crazy is sexy as hell so there's that.

I snagged my phone from the nightstand and silenced the alarm before rolling over to Trent's side of the bed, but he was already gone and the bed was cold. This was not all that unusual. Life with a homicide detective for a boyfriend was anything but a banker's hours. I often go to bed alone or wake up to an empty bed when my guy has been called out to fight crime and hunt killers at all hours of the night.

Especially if he was called out for a fresh one early this morning while I was still asleep. In fact, I was such a heavy sleeper that there really wasn't much that could wake me up. Granny always said it's like trying to raise the dead. Again, another sparkling review. It was like my very own Yelp page up in here. Who needed enemies when you had close friends and family, am I right?

Trent, on the other hand, was a very light sleeper. Whether it was from his time as an Army Ranger or with the police department, I didn't know. I just knew that the slightest noise had him popping out of bed like a Jack in the Box. So, when I realized Trent was long gone already, it didn't surprise me.

I pushed myself up to sit on the side of the bed and let the room stop spinning. One day, I swear I will learn that tequila is the devil's premium adult beverage.

Unfortunately, that day was not today. You would've thought I'd know better by now, but no, I did not.

I remembered when I was nineteen and a freshman in college, my parents were out of town and I invited some friends over. I had even given my boyfriend at the time—a real winner, if you ask me, but then again, I could always pick the boy that would be nothing but trouble out of a lineup and then date him anywhere from six months to four years—money for alcohol to give to a friend of his that I had never met before. Because that's what all smart girls did. I would learn later that this friend was a girl and they were banging on the side. But I wouldn't find that out until months later. In the moment she seemed cool and she had a friendly smile. I liked her.

But I digress.

Imagine my surprise when my boyfriend not only showed up with the alcohol, but also forty-five of his closest friends. He thought a party meant a rager in my parents' house. Fan-freaking-tastic. First, my friends and I hid in the dark with all the lights off, but then he kept calling and calling. Homie blew up my phone until I finally answered and admitted that his many "friends" would not be allowed inside. I did, however, tell him that I would like the alcohol that I had paid for. It was then he decided he would stay with me and my friends instead of his. I should have realized then that he was an alcoholic, but at this point, I was just glad he wasn't the guy who jizzed on my prom dress. Later, I would break up with him over his wandering dick and James would be there to be my white knight who picked up the pieces.

That night, I did tequila shots like a boss. Unfortunately, I had never drank tequila or any other type of alcohol before. But in true Shelby fashion, I would go big or go home. The next day, I wanted to die. But I didn't.

I also didn't learn any lessons, because here I was this morning, waiting to die from my hangover straight from the third circle of hell. Why I do this to myself like once or twice a year is beyond me. I am such a fucking idiot. I will never learn.

So when my alarm sounded in the stillness of the early morning—and real talk, 8:00 a.m. is early after a night of imbibing in tequila and debauchery—I seriously considered throwing it out the window. Unfortunately for me, that wouldn't have worked, because Missy decided she's a dog these days and loved to play fetch. Cranky bitch would have just brought it back as it squawked in the room. So instead, I silenced it and decided I needed to pour a pot of coffee in my face in order to maybe survive the Oompah band that had taken up residence in my brain. But again, only time would tell.

Once the room stopped spinning, I pushed up to stand and padded barefoot into the kitchen as saliva pooled in my mouth, and I prayed to Jesus and all the baby angels—literally anyone who would listen—not to let me hurl.

I had to stop in the doorway of the kitchen and cling to the wall for a second and close my eyes tight to make sure I was steady on my feet and not still swaying like a tree branch in a strong breeze. When I could open my eyes again, I would make coffee.

Trent was old school when it came to his coffee. He swore it wasn't really coffee unless you could eat it with a fork like some kind of caffeinated mashed potatoes. I assumed this was another leftover Army quirk, so I ignored it. I also liked coffee, so I went along with this plan on a normal day. Brewing coffee in a Mr. Coffee pot didn't trip me out, but today I needed coffee and fast and was definitely missing my old Keurig that he had tossed out when he brought back his first love, the coffee carafe.

I grabbed the glass carafe from the plate under the coffeemaker and filled it with water before dumping it all down into the reservoir on the back, all while cursing Trent for not leaving me any freaking coffee.

That bastard!

Sadly, things went awry when I popped the lid off the can of coffee grounds. I went to scoop them into the coffeemaker, when the scent of shitty coffee hit my nose and all that tequila and whatever the hell else I had consumed the night before made an alarming recurrence. It was all I could do to make it to the kitchen sink before my stomach released its contents.

I ran the faucet and splashed the cool water on my face before cupping some in my hand to rinse out my mouth. That was unfortunate. I was hoping I could rally, but really by that point, I just wanted to curl up on the cold stone tile and wait to die.

I had finally gotten the coffee percolating, pulled the carafe from the coffeemaker before the pot was done, and filled a mug before replacing the carafe—a bad habit of mine but whatever. I chugged the coffee like I was shot-gunning a beer at an outdoor music festival and prayed the caffeine would stop my pulse from sounding in my skull on repeat.

I was flopped over the cool stone top of the kitchen counter with the side of my face pressed to the granite and my hand still wrapped around my coffee mug when my phone rang, making me flinch. Nope, still not back in action, which was a bummer, because I was just starting to feel human again—well, at least a little bit.

"Hello?" I answered when I blindly slid my finger across the screen of my phone to unlock it before lifting it to my ear. I didn't even bother to look to see who was calling or to lift my head from its resting place on the countertop.

"Shelby, my girl," Granny said through the phone. "Why do you sound so weird?"

"I think I died and no one bothered to tell me," I answered. God, I hope I don't hurl again. I really hate throwing up. I actually try to avoid it at all costs.

And then my dear, sweet grandmother had the nerve to laugh. "You never did have my constitution," she said like a jerk. "You take after your grandfather. He was kind of a candy ass when it came to tequila. Cute in his uniform with a dynamite ass, but a total lightweight. He liked to drink big pussy drinks that came in hollowed out pineapples with umbrellas and fruit skewers in them."

"Thanks, I think," I mumble to myself more than anyone else.

"What are you doing today?" she asked me as she changes the subject quickly. If I was feeling more like myself, I would have known that I shouldn't have trusted her quick one-eighty.

"Dying?" I answered on a question because I'm not really sure that I'm going to make it out of this kitchen alive yet.

"No, for real?" Granny asked, trying to get me to stay on topic, and I let out a groan.

"I am for real," I told her. "I feel like hammered horse shit."

"You probably look like it too," she added saucily. "So clean yourself up and come over here for a Pleasures Party. It'll be fun!"

Then I really groaned. I loved my granny, but I wasn't so sure I could handle a roomful of octogenarians and their favorite marital aids.

"Uhh . . . I don't know about that, Granny," I hedged. "I don't feel so hot."

"Nonsense!" she shouted down the line, making me cringe as the volume of her voice ricocheted around in my brain. "Get dressed and get over here pronto. I'll make you my world famous hangover buster."

"Uhh . . ."

"See you in thirty!" she hollered before disconnecting.

"Well." I sighed. "Alrighty then."

I had thirty minutes to get there and was planning on being fashionably late, so I pushed myself up and poured myself another cup of coffee and popped some bread in the toaster. This time, I took a moment to doctor the cup the way I really liked it—with ridiculous amounts of flavored coffee creamer—and I'm not gonna lie; that first sip was fantastic.

My toast popped and I grabbed it with my hands

while shouting "Ooohh, hot, hot," before dropping it on a plate.

When I was done and it looked like my breakfast of champions was going to stay where I put it, I placed my cup and my plate in the sink and made my way down the hall, back to the bedroom, and on through to the bathroom. I cranked up the water in the shower to near scalding temperatures. I needed to sweat out all of the tequila and bad decisions and then wash it all—and if the crusty stuff on my side was anything to go by, some other things a lady wouldn't name—off my body and down the drain.

I scrubbed every inch of myself twice before turning off the taps and grabbing a towel from the rack. I made my way into the closet and grabbed a pair of lavender lace panties Trent liked so much I had to beg him not to tear them the last time I wore them, and their matching bra that did spectacular things for my boobs. I stepped into a pair of denim shorts and then layered a lavender tank top over a white one. The weatherman said it was going to be a hot one today, and I wanted to bask in it. This was my favorite kind of day.

I slid my diamond studs through my ears and layered small gold chains with little charms hanging from them around my neck before going back to the mirror in the bathroom to brush my teeth. I took one look at my face and cringed. I still looked pretty green around the gills, so I decided to wear a full-coverage foundation and powder to combat that. I dusted some bronzer and a sweet peach blush on my face to add a little healthy color, even if it was fake, and then I dabbed a little dark brown mascara on my lashes before deeming myself good enough.

I stuffed my wallet, cellphone, and lip balm in a tiny, brown hobo purse and slid it up my arm before slipping my feet into a pair of brown flip-flops and heading out the door.

I beeped the locks on my little white Jeep and climbed behind the wheel. The morning sun shining bright made me want to crawl into a hole and die, so I slipped my oversized Kate Spade sunglasses onto my face and lowered the visor as I drove to Granny's downtown high-rise.

I'm only about twenty-five minutes late when I pull up to the valet check at the front of the building, over-all, a good turn out for me. I signed in at the front desk before making my way to the elevator banks. Luck was on my side this morning as an elevator dinged and opened its doors before I ever hit the call button, and I rode it by myself to the tenth floor, where my Granny was waiting for me with her door open.

Present

"Holy Cock-a-doodle-doo, Batman," I say, more than a little stunned when Granny ushers me into her apart-ment that has been completely transformed.

"I know!" she says excitedly. "Awesome, right?"

"So... *uhh*... awesome."

"It really is," she gushes.

"There's dongs for days in here," I add, letting the words fall right out of my mouth before I can censor them, and my granny laughs.

"I know," she says on a laugh. "Isn't it great?"

"So great," I repeat her assessment and I'm not real sure that I mean it. I think that I'm in shock from the ridiculous array of fake cocks that now line my grandmother's apartment. There are pink ones, yellow once, peach ones, black ones, long ones, short ones, glittery ones, glass ones. It's like a tornado blew through and now I am in an Oz of dicks and my grandmother is the wizard.

"Now come on in so we can do it up right," she orders as she pushes open the door wider so that I can pass through.

I take another look around. Her living room is full of old ladies and a variety of dildos in every size and color, and I don't mean flesh tones. While there are those too, there are also bright-colored cocks in yellows, blues, and purples, and there is even a pink glittery one that catches my eye.

"Do it up right?" I ask, feeling confused. The giant dicks have clearly turned my brain to mush.

"You know, like we did in Korea for Sophie, but bigger and more dicks," Granny explains.

"Huh?"

"You have to know that you and Trent are on the fast track to Holy Matrimony," she says as she shoots me the side eye. I'm not sure that she's saying that it's amazing that Trent and I are together, or if she's asking if I can really be so dense that I didn't see how close Trent and I had grown.

"That's right," Marla chimes in. "We figure if Kane went all caveman on sweet Sophia, then Trent is going to want to lock this down and soon."

"Oh," I say, finally clueing in. "I don't know . . ."

But I do. They're not wrong. Trent and I have been going strong for two years now. We are deep in the love bubble, and his cock is deep in me almost every night. I have been secretly dreaming about my wedding to Marla's grandson ever since we got back from Korea, and by the way she's looking at me now, she just might have some pertinent inside information on my marital situation. So I sit my ass down and let my grandmother and her friends wow me with their knowledge of sex toys.

Granny places a tall glass of what looks like mud in front of me proclaiming that it was "the hair of the dog," and I eyed it suspiciously. I even think I see and egg or two floating around in it. "It's better if you just shoot it back."

So I do.

After a while I feel better. A day listening to these women who were all married for years has me laughing so hard I think I might pee my pants and my ears burning but it was also exactly what I needed. These ladies really enjoy their lives. When it's time for me to go home I thank them all for their time and hug my grandmother.

"Maybe you should take Big Thunder home with you," Marla says as if she's trying to be helpful.

I eye Big Thunder dubiously.

I am already loaded down with a variety of dildos, vibrators, lube, a sex swing, tie downs, handcuffs, and—against my wishes—a long string of anal beads.

"Hell no," I say finally. "That big, purple dick is liable to split me right in two."

The room of old ladies busts out laughing.

"Well all right, dear," Marla says with a wicked twinkle in her eyes. "You'll just have to settle for my grandson."

"Life with Trent is anything but settling," I reply softly.

"I knew I liked you," she tells me as she hugs me goodbye. "See you later."

"Enjoy the good dick!" Granny shouts from within her apartment, and I can't help but laugh as I make my way down the hall to the elevator bank. I'm still feeling a little rough, so I decide to spend the rest of the day indulging in my favorite things—magazines, junk food, and Bravo—with my favorite cat.

But you know what they say about best-laid plans and all that...

CHAPTER 5

HAPPILY EVER AFTER AND A LITTLE HAIR OF THE DOG

"Thank you," I say to the kid working the valet as I hand him my ticket after he brings my little white Jeep around.

"See you around," he replies as he gives me the up and down. We're probably around the same age; maybe I'm a year or two older than him. He's cute, but I'm apparently the kind of girl that likes a guy with handcuffs and the ability to arrest me for my own good. Even though that fun little stunt of his really pissed me off, Trent is the only guy for me.

"Bye." I smile as I hop in the driver seat and shut the door behind me.

I adjust the seat back to the height of an average-sized person. Sometimes, I wonder if it's an unknown rule that all men who work valet also be an appropriate size to play professional basketball. Now, I'm a normal height at like five feet, seven inches, but every time I get in a car after it's been valeted, I have to reset every-thing. It's wild. I wonder where they find these guys. Or even if it's in the "Now Hiring" listing for the job that they must rival the height of a redwood tree.

I roll down my windows, punch the button to crank up my stereo, and Taylor Swift's "Blank Space" blares through the speakers. The volume makes we wince, and I immediately turn it down. Maybe my hangover is not completely gone after all. I tug at the neckline of my shirt to get a little more air flowing as I've start-ed to sweat like a sinner in church. I roll my window down and crank up the air conditioner.

And maybe I should take it easy for the rest of the day.

In fact, that is exactly what I'm going to do.

Instead of getting on the highway to head to my condo, I turn on my blinker and stop at the red light be-fore turning right toward the shopping center. There's an Albertson's at the far end of this shopping center. I need a little hair of the dog, or at least a gallon of ice cream, some tabloid magazines, and some terrible television to make my world right again. That coupled with about twelve hours of sleep and a vow to God himself that I will never partake of the Devil's tequila again and this hangover might just be behind me.

I pull into a parking space, grab the keys from the ignition, and beep the locks, dropping my keys into my pocketbook. I make my way into the grocery store before grabbing a shopping cart from the row of them by the front door. I look to the produce section before being real with myself.

I'm not going to buy fruit—maybe some strawberry topping for my ice cream sundae, but not actual fruits and vegetables. That is *not* the cure for a tequila hangover. I need grease and fat and sugar to cure what ails me. And if that still doesn't work, maybe a little hair of the dog. I'd hate to touch the devil's tonic again so soon but I'm feeling miserable again. The fun I was having with Granny and the girls distracted me, but now, I kind of just want to curl up on my sofa with a comfy blanket and a bottle of ibuprofen.

So I just keep on walking on to the frozen food section. I pull open the glass door and pluck a carton of my favorite rocky road ice cream and a carton of mint chocolate chip for posterity. It's good to keep things interesting. Variety is the spice of life after all.

I make my way to the checkout counter by way of the candy aisle for a variety of chocolate, and I pass by the magazine section, which is when I fall down the rabbit hole. The bridal magazines are staring me in the eye, and they are the little devil on my shoulder telling me I'm going to be the prettiest bride ever in the whole history of the entire world and that my wedding to Trent will be the most fabulous in all the land, so I need to buy them right now.

And I do.

I listen to that little devil on my shoulder and scoop up all of the bridal magazines that I can get my hot little hands on like a Columbian Drug Lord smuggling my wares across the border. I'm like the creepy guy in "Lord of the Rings" coveting my pretties.

I buy them all.

Brides. Modern Brides. California Brides.

And *Exotic Birds*, because I was excitable, and

it had the right letters but the wrong categories. The magazines were ordered alphabetically and I wouldn't realize it until much, much later. It happens.

I push my cart up to the cashier, tagging an extra-large bottle of pain reliever on my way by and start unloading my boon onto the conveyor belt while minding my own business—*like one should*—when the man in line behind me snickers loudly like a jerk. He comments on my purchases as if he has a place to do so, and I am way too hung over for this bullshit.

"All you're missing is the chocolate cake and the tampons," he says on a laugh.

"And the shotgun shells," I add with a sickeningly sweet smile on my face and a roll of my eyes.

"Why would you need shotgun shells?" he replies. His confusion is showing on his face.

"To chase away fuckers intent on butting their noses into other people's business when they are hung over and avoiding tequila at all costs because it is the devil's juice box. So I'm going to need you to not comment on my life while I'm trying to be one with the Lord here. Now, move along!"

"Sheesh," he mutters as he moves his cart to another checkout aisle. "Crazy PMS-ing bitches."

"And I don't have PMS!" I shout through the grocery store. I cringe at the volume of my own voice. It's loud and shrill. I sound like a psycho as I my voice carries throughout the front of the grocery store. I lower my gaze in an effort to minimize my humiliation but not making eye contact with anyone else. If I can't see them, they can't see me, right?

I turn back to my shopping cart and finish unloading all my candy, ice cream, and carefully selected wedding magazines. And also, the bird one, but I'm not willing to admit my mistake at this particular juncture in life, It's been a brutal enough shopping excursion and I don't want to add any more insult to my injury sundae so I just load them all up on the conveyor belt before glancing up. It's then I realize I have drawn an audience. Everyone around me is staring. Conversations have completely stopped.

Well, damn.

Apparently, I caused a bit of a stir.

"What?" I ask the room at large.

"Nothing," the checker says softly before she begins scanning my items.

"Sure, sure," I mutter absentmindedly as each item beeps across the red light.

"So, when is the big day?" she asks me, and this is one of those moments I really wish I was paying more attention, because then I would realize she was asking me when I was getting married. Which, who the hell knows? It's not like Trent has asked me—*yet*. But hopefully soon-ish. And I can't answer that question with "hopefully soon," so instead I say the most profound thing possible.

"Huh?" I ask with an obviously confused expression on my face. Mensa, eat your hearts out.

"When are you getting married?" she rephrases her question as she waves a magazine in front of my face—a wedding one, not the bird one.

"Oh," I answer awkwardly. "We haven't set a date yet."

"Cool," she says as she chucks them into a bag.

"It'll be $87.65."

Jesus H. Christ wedding magazines are expensive. Don't these fuckers know that we'll still have a wedding to pay for after we take out a small loan for these magazines? I hand her some bills and accept my change with a smile on my face as I say, "Thank you."

One thing working at the home improvement store taught me is that you should never treat someone in the service industry rudely. The things people demanded or asked for when I worked at the customer service desk were terrible. I could not get moved to the custom kitchens and baths department fast enough, and even those people were lunatics. I remember this one lady wanted a double kitchen and wanted to price match it based on some sketchy website sale overseas. Uhh . . . no, ma'am. We don't do that here.

"Have a good one," I tell her as I grab the handle of my shopping cart and push it through the sliding glass doors and out into the hot parking lot. While weather is usually perfect in San Diego and all that, it still gets pretty hot in the summer.

I palm my keys and beep the locks on my key fob. I open the tailgate and load my bounty into the trunk before depositing the cart in the return. I hop in the driver seat and head for home. I'm excited to hunker down with a little comfort and hope for the future because any future with Trent is bound to be a beautiful thing.

I love summers in San Diego, with the sun shining in the blue sky filled with white, wispy clouds. I love all of the palm trees that are not indigenous to California. I love it all. I cannot imagine myself living anywhere else in the world, so I roll down my windows and let the cool summer breeze roll off the ocean before it disappears and the heat remains again as I drive up the highway to my little condo complex. Daisy and Alyssa are pulling out of the front gate as I'm pulling in, and she beeps her horn, making me laugh as I wave to them.

I pull into my covered parking space with my unit number painted on the curb and put the Jeep in Park before tossing my purse over my shoulder and grab my groceries from the trunk. When you live in a condo complex like this one, your assigned space is a ways away from your unit, so I have gotten accustomed to carrying everything in one go. I keep a large tote bag that was a free gift with purchase at Victoria's Secret in the back to put all of my groceries in so that I can carry them all at once. There is no way I'm making more than one trip back to this car.

Ain't nobody got time for that.

I loop the handles of the bags over my arm and head down to the mailboxes on my way through the complex. I use the keys on my keychain to unlock my mailbox, when my creepy puppy neighbor, Steve, walks up. He's not really that bad; I just think he is a little lonely. And when he's lonely, he likes to steal my Victoria's Secret catalogue and circle the items he thinks I should acquire for myself. And sometimes, when he's really bored, he peeps in my windows when I'm changing. Trent isn't real wild about it, but he's mostly harmless. *I think.*

"Hey, Shelby," he says to me.

"Hey, Steve. What's happening?" I ask offering him a warm smile. Steve is like a lonely puppy. He needs kindness, attention, and frequent walks or else he will shit in your closet and chew up all of your shoes.

"Not too much," he replies while looking expectantly at the stack of mail in my hands. "Get anything good in the mail?"

"Probably not," I tell him honestly. "There's nothing exciting going on around here these days."

"Famous last words," he says on an awkward laugh making a shiver run down my spine. My granny would say that someone just stepped on my grave and I hope to God that she would be wrong but now I can't help but feel a sense of foreboding in the air. I can't help but pray that things continue on their incredibly boring path. Too bad I wouldn't have my prayers answered tonight.

"Yeah," I say feeling that sense of dread rise up in my stomach.

"Are you still seeing that cop?" he asks, changing the subject quickly.

"Yeah, Trent and I are still together," I answer.

"Oh, okay," he says. "So, there was a woman here looking for you." But that's it. That's all the information that Steve provides. He's helpful like that.

"Oh, who was it?" I ask as I flip through my mail, taking a quick look at the bills and adverts in the stack.

"Some blonde," he says. "I wasn't really paying attention."

"Did she say her name?" I ask. The only blonde I know is Sophie and she was revisiting her last seven meals when I talked to her last, so I highly doubt that it was her.

"No." Well, that was helpful.

"Did she leave a message? Maybe say if she would be back?" I ask.

"No." I hold in a sigh. Steve is great if you want to know how you look in a pair of thigh highs but not if you have actual important information to obtain.

"Oh," I respond. "Well, okay. I have to go, but I'll see you around."

"I'll see you around, sweet Shelby," he mimics on a leery wink.

My thoughts are lost on settling into my pajamas and scooping out a major sundae. Not on whoever the woman was who came looking for me.

Too bad it's like Steve said—famous last words. Yet I wouldn't realize that until a little later. But by then, it would be way too late.

CHAPTER 6

ARRESTED DEVELOPMENT

"Merrrooow," my cat, Missy, calls out to me as I push open the front door to my condo.

"Hello, my pretty girl," I coo to her. She is the best cat ever. James's mom had a cat that had a litter while we were in college right around the time that my childhood dog passed away. I was so sad that he brought me over to hold the kittens. He said it was important for me to see the circle of life and hold it in my hands. He felt it was important to remember that there needed to be death to make way for new life. I held Missy in my hands and I just knew that we were meant to be together. I was lucky that his mom let me keep her because she never really liked me anyways. That should have been a big freaking red flag, but whatever. That thought makes me nervous because I haven't met Trent's mom yet. She lives in New Jersey with the rest of his family. I hope she likes me. I don't know what

I would do if she didn't. Would Trent still want to be with me? Yikes. Those are some heavy thoughts for a hangover day so I push them away for another day.

I make my way to my house and use my key to open the door. I drop my purse and my mail on the table by the door that I had found on double clearance at World Market right after I bought this place. I had these neat little details by the legs, and I could just tell that it would look perfect in this space. It makes the perfect entryway space to set things for safe keeping on my way in or out of the house. I head into the kitchen to put my ice cream in the freezer. Ripping open the bag of M&M's, and of course, with my luck the bag pops open in an explosion of epic proportions and M&M's ping around the kitchen as the skip and then land who the hell knows where. I let out a frustrated sigh and start picking them up. Missy bats a few of them around. I don't worry about her eating them because her love is for cans of wet cat food and tuna. Everything else could go to hell for all she cares. I pop a few in my mouth as I go before washing my hands. Hey, ten second rule!

I crack open a can of cat food that smells like holy hell and rotting fish all in one, spooning it into Missy's little ceramic bowl with a pink princess crown painted into the bottom. I want to gag, and the stench is turning my stomach a bit, but Missy is more than pleased with the situation, if the way she is twitching her tail and her twisting around my legs is anything to go by.

I I crack open a can and scoop out a big chunk of the foul smelling food that she loves so much and place her bowl on the floor. She falls on it with a weird but cute little "Eep!"

I open up one of the upper cabinets and pull down a cereal bowl. I love the Pioneer Woman dishes and bought a mishmash of different patterns. I like having an eclectic mix of things around me in my nest and for me it works. Matchy-matching stuff is so boring!

I embrace the cool air from the freezer when I pull open the door to grab the tub of mint chocolate chip ice cream. Scooping some—read: I scooped a shit-ton—into a bowl, I top it with an excessive amount of chocolate syrup and M&M's that I had salvaged from the explosion.

I tuck my stack of magazines under my arm before picking up my bowl and grabbing a spoon from the drawer. Missy is still face-down and ass-up in her little kitty princess bowl, so she couldn't care less as I leave the room.

I walk back through the open doorway into the living room and set my bowl of ice cream on the coffee table. I pick up the remote and turn on the television. I settle into the sofa as I click through the channels looking for anything I can just enjoy. And my luck holds out when I hit Bravo and see there is an all-day *Real Housewives* marathon.

I flip open the first magazine on top of the stack before noticing the bright green parrot with yellow feathers on his forehead and blue tips on his wings on the cover. It's then I realize it's all about exotic birds of the Amazon. This bird is kind of pretty, and I wonder if *I* should get a bird. It might be nice to have another animal in the house.

And then I hear a little kitty battle cry from the

other room followed by the sounds of all the cooking utensils being thrown off the kitchen counters. I hear the *thwop thwop thwop* of bird wings as a small sparrow flies into the living room with Missy hot on its heels.

I'm not sure what to do or what makes me think of it, but I jump off the sofa and sprint over to the front door, pull it open real fast so that the bird can fly out, but then slam it closed so Missy can't get out. Missy is *not* an outside cat. Missy is the kind of cat that eats canned cat food out of a hand painted china bowl. She's the kind of cat that likes to be brushed regularly and have her claws professionally filed. She likes to sleep on a silk cushion or Trent's king-sized bed not some back alley. Some days, I'm not even sure she's actually a cat. She's like some kind of princess from a faraway land who expects everyone to wait on her hand and foot. Because I know for a fact that she could not survive in the wild.

"Me-rower," Missy pouts, because I won't let her out to chase the bird.

"No, Missy." I roll my eyes. I mean really. She's not going anywhere. She has never hunted anything a day in her life. I'm not sure what's gotten into her.

"Meee-ooow!" she challenges me. Missy is like a temperamental pre-teen. She always throws a fit when she doesn't get her way. One time, I told her that it wasn't time for wet food when she sat on the counter and started begging. She responded by using her front paw to fling things off the counter to smash on the floor. To say we were both unhappy was an understatement.

"Ugh," I groan. I have no idea why she is being so

difficult when what I really should be doing is wonder how the hell a fucking parrot got into my condo to begin with. Where I live, there are a lot of trees around the property and a flock of wild parrots who nest in the trees. It's rumored that twenty years ago, a woman's apartment building was on fire and the fire department couldn't get all of her parrots out so they opened up the doors of all of the cages and then flung the windows open so they could escape into the night. As the story goes, those parrots not only survived, but went wild and continued to populate the San Diego area for generations to come. But I still have no idea how in the hell one came to be inside *my* condo.

I also don't put much thought into it either, so I sit my ass down on the sofa and toss the bird magazine aside. I would figure out much later when I wasn't so tired that a tiny bird couldn't have let itself into my home that someone else had to. The thought that someone else who wasn't meant to be here had invaded my safe sanctuary would never once cross my mind, not until it was too late. But for now, I'm too hungover and to focused on my future impending nuptials.

I guess we are just not meant to expand our little family right now. I don't think I could handle anyone else but Missy. Trent talks off and on about getting a dog, but I don't know if we're ready for that. Maybe we should get a plant first. If we can take care of a plant then we can get a dog. Missy doesn't count because everyone knows that cats mostly take care of themselves. And hopefully babies won't come for some time. My cousin, Sky, who lives in South Dakota has a baby. She's adorable and everything, but I can barely take care of myself right now, let alone another person.

I fold my legs up underneath me to sit crisscross applesauce and open another magazine. I flip through page after page of wedding dresses—and then—*there it is*. It's beautiful. It's a cream strapless with a sweetheart neckline. It laces up the back in a heavy cream satin bow. A soft rose pattern is delicately embroidered over the bust, and the skirt falls in soft, fluffy waves from a basque waist. The entire chiffon confection would fit my curves perfectly, and all at once, in my head, I see myself walking down the aisle to Trent.

This is it.

This is my wedding dress.

I have chills just looking at it. I always heard that when you know, you know. And this is my know. This is my dress and Trent is my guy. I just know that when we plan the rest of it, everything will fall into place. Now, I just need the groom to fucking propose. But all things in good time, and all that bullshit. I know in my heart that Trent and I are meant to be. When I think about it, I want to see his last name tacked onto mine. I want to hold babies with his dark hair and green eyes—*eventually*. I want a lifetime with Trent, and I know that I am going to get it.

Based on what Marla was hinting at heavily today, a proposal is imminent. I cannot wait. I set my magazine down and pick up my bowl of ice cream while I get lost with the *Beverly Hills* girls for a bit. Those chicks are crazy and I fucking love it. Trent thinks the Dames and I are nuts but we have nothing on this banana sandwich business.

The two girls on the show who are always a little

over the top are fight about some apple juice dog and something about Boy George. I could totally be friends with Boy George. The other ladies are running around being total nut bags , when there's a knock at the door.

I don't bother to look to see who it is. It could be anyone from Daisy and Alyssa to Trent. Although Trent has his own key so he wouldn't knock. But there isn't anyone else I could think of that might come looking for me this late into the afternoon. I guess it could be whoever it was that was looking for me earlier. Who knows? But I don't bother myself worrying about them. I just unlock the door and swing it open.

And immediately wish I hadn't.

Standing on my front porch are several uniformed officers. None of whom I recognize, which is wild, because by now, I know just about everyone. It's weird that people I know wouldn't come here if something was wrong. I look around and see Kane is standing just past the officers who knocked on the door.

"Shelby," he says to me. "Can you step out here please?"

"Sure," I say, not even caring that I'm wearing the smallest pair of knit booty shorts, ones I'm sure haven't fit since 2003, the white tank top I wore under a blue one earlier, and no bra, because home is where the bras and pants are not. Taking them off is always the main event in my getting comfortable because I am finally home routine. They are probably strewn around my apartment because I don't even think about doing it at this point, I just do it out of habit.

"You have the right to remain silent," he says in a firm voice.

"Wait, what?" I gasp and feel my eyes glaze over. I couldn't have heard Kane correctly. This is Kane. Kane is my friend. He's married to one of my closest girlfriends. He is Trent's partner on the force and once saw me naked and unconscious in my kitchen after Trent scared me and I ran into the glass slider before blacking out. He wouldn't be arresting me, right?

"Shelby," Kane calls out while snapping his fingers in front of my face to get my attention. I must have drifted off. Clearly, I am in an alternate universe because he can't possibly be here to arrest me. "Are you listening to me?"

And I'm not. Not really.

I'm so confused. One minute, I was in my condo watching *The Real Housewives of Beverly Hills*—one of my greatest guilty pleasures that I like to partake of from time to time—and eating ice cream while looking at my secret stash of bridal magazines.

I know, I know. I shouldn't be buying them until I have a ring on my finger, but I couldn't help myself. My mom says it's bad luck to buy the magazines before you wear a man's ring, kind of like putting the cart before the horse, but I know it's coming.

I can feel it.

Ever since we got back from Korea, where Kane and Sophie got hitched in a surprise wedding—surprise for Kane because it was spur of the moment, surprise for Sophie because Kane didn't tell her they had gotten married until the tea was spilled in the news—something has been different with Trent. He has the look of a man wanting to be tied down. He's ready and so am I.

And I know their marriage wasn't conventional,

per se, but it was romantic as hell when you stop and think about it—Kane going all alpha badass caveman and tricking Sophie into marrying him so he wouldn't ever have to live without her. I think deep down, we all just want to be loved like that.

I would give anything, and I do mean *anything*, for Trent to carry me over his alpha badass shoulder to the altar, but mark my words, there will be an altar. I am not eloping. I have waited too goddamn long to find the man of my dreams. I put up with one douche canoe boyfriend after the next until the last one took the cake when he not only cheated on me, but beat the crap out of me too. As if it was my fault his cock slipped and fell into my best friend at the time. Fucker. And Trent and I have definitely had our ups and downs too. Our road to wedded bliss and a Target registry hasn't been paved with lilies but it was ours and I wouldn't want it any other way. Well . . . except for that time that he accidentally—so he says—pushed me into an open grave when I wouldn't go out with him. But in my defense, I was still feeling pretty raw from my relationship with James and I was in no way looking for a new man in my life. I was gun shy, so sue me.

But I know it's coming . . . or at least I thought it was. Now, maybe I'm not so sure.

Trent and I have been in a really good place. We haven't fought at all, and I haven't wormed my way into any of his investigations in a really long time, so that should earn me perfect fiancée material points, right?

At least *I* think it does.

Not to mention, Trent and I have been banging like

bunnies since we got back. We've been burning up the sheets not only late at night, but early in the morning too. And I'm not gonna lie, sometimes in the middle of the day when we meet for lunch at the Jewish delicatessen, he follows me into the ladies' room and we have a quickie on the counter. Our chemistry is hotter than ever and we can't get enough of each other. I know I will never not want Trent the way that I do.

So when a knock sounded on my front door, I answered it. I wasn't sure who was coming over, but life in the fast lane with the Dangerous Dames could mean anything. Not to mention my two favorite former hookers live around the corner in the next building over and stop on by from time to time to borrow a cup of vodka or a disguise.

What? It's not like we bake or some shit.

But when I answered the door, it wasn't Daisy and Alyssa wanting to catch up over some crappy television programming, or even my grandmother and her bestie after a night on the town in some "borrowed" wheels that they lifted off of Marla's boyfriend, Hal. It was Kane and Trent and a bunch of uniformed officers. And no one was smiling.

For a second, I hadn't seen Trent, because he was standing at the back of the pack—which was also odd, come to think of it—not front and center and I thought maybe Trent had been hurt on the job. San Diego is a great city that I love with all of my heart. I never want to live anywhere else, but it also has its share of crime, and life as a homicide detective is always dangerous. I worry for the day when I will get the phone call that something has happened to Trent on the job. And if that day ever comes it will gut me, but I have always known that it is a possibility and if I want to be with him, I need to be at peace with that.

Although, I'm not quite sure of what is actually happening here. So when I look over Kane's shoulders to Trent, I see him look at me. His clover green eyes that have burned into mine while he slid deep into my body on more than one occasion burn me now—only not in a good way.

What the hell is happening here?

"Trent?" I ask him, but he doesn't answer. In fact, Trent turns and walks away. "Trent? What's going on?"

I move to follow him out the door, but Kane puts a hand up to stop me as two uniformed officers step up behind him to help intercede me. And I am not gonna lie, they strike an intimidating figure.

"Shelby, look at me," Kane says, and I jerk my gaze from Trent's retreating form back to Kane's handsome face.

"What's going on, Kane?" I ask him this time.

"You have the right to remain silent. Anything you say can and will be held against you in a court of law. You have the right to an attorney. If you cannot afford one, one will be provided to you by the State," Kane says to me in a firm voice, one I have never heard from him before. He is always my friend, Kane, but I have the sinking feeling that here today, he is Detective Green as he reads me my Miranda Rights. I have never, in all the fun and mostly harmless trouble that I have cooked up in my life, have I ever had my rights read to me before. And I'm suddenly feeling a little scared. "Do you understand these rights as I have presented them to you?"

"Yes," I whisper as they turn me around and frisk me. "But I don't understand what you think I've done."

"Shelby Whitmore, you are under arrest for the murder of James Alexander," he says as the metal cuffs snick closed over my wrists.

Well, I did not see that one coming.

Too bad I didn't do it . . .

CHAPTER 7

JAILHOUSE ROCK

"**D**o you think Elvis Presley had to deal with scratchy wool blankets while he was singing 'Jailhouse Rock'?" I ask my lovely cellmate.

I mean really. I itch all over. It could be because this is a freaking jail cell and I'm in the middle of a huge panic attack over all of the germs that could be crawling all over the place. I'm not that big of a princess that I need the county lock up to be like the Four Seasons, but still, this is terrible. I don't even like to camp. I had a boyfriend take me camping once in high school and I thought we were going to be all cute and shit and I will tell you, we were not! We were hot and sweaty and smelly. And he even expected me to pee on the side of a mountain. I tried once, peed in my shoe and then started my period and demanded to go home. I eye the stainless steel toilet that sits in the middle of the room in front of God and everyone. I better not start my freaking period this week.

"Probably not," Evanna answers. "The King was a god. He could totally do whatever he wanted. Even if he was in jail."

"I find that fascinating. If I still had my phone, I would google him and see if her ever was arrested," I tell her. Apparently, my new cell mate is a super fan of *The King*. She has been spouting off Elvis Presley facts ever since I was dumped in this cell with her.

"Elvis Presley was arrested on October 18, 1956 for a bar fight," she recites like the fount of rock 'n' roll information that she apparently is. It's super impressive in a kind of adorably creepy way. I'm just hoping that she doesn't turn out to be a serial killer. I have enough on my plate right now that I really can't deal with being skinned and made into a suit. My skin is kind of fabulous though. I work hard to take extra good care of it so when I'm sixty I'll still look fabulous. "But the charges were dropped the next day and the manager made a public apology."

"Good to know," I respond as I sit back on the cot and wonder about all the bugs and bacteria that have to be swirling all around this place while she keeps rattling on stats and random fun facts about the Graceland God. This place is probably a veritable cesspool. God, I hope I don't get shanked in here. Last time, I was with my BFF, Daisy, even though she wasn't my bestie back then. She was so kind and sweet and funny. I know that she took care of me and kept the rougher girls away from me when she realized I was an innocent—like not a criminal, not all Madonna style like a virgin.

"Did you know that he was a twin?" she asks me

when I see Trent walk by. He looks tired and I can see the dark circles under his eyes from here, but good. His dark hair is messy like he has been running his hands through it like he does when he's agitated. His jeans and t-shirt are rumpled like he slept in them. I know that he didn't because he slept next to me and I can testify that he was very naked so he must have pulled them off of the floor when he got up in the morning. It makes me think he got a call out in the middle of the night and has been going ever since. It makes me want to reach and out and comfort him, but I don't.

I need him.

I need Trent to unlock these doors and pull me into his arms. I need him to tell me that everything is going to be alright when I can't help but feel like everything is all wrong. I need him to tell me what to do so I call out to him before he passes by. He's not even looking at me. It's like he doesn't even know that I am here.

"Trent!" I shout as I hop off the cot and run to the front of the cell. "Trent!"

He looks up and glances at me as I cling to the bars, begging for him to come to me and tell me this is all a dream, that this is all some colossal mistake and I'm not really charged with a murder I didn't commit. I need to know what to do to make this all go away. That everything will go back to the way that it was before I got drunk in that bar and threatened my douche ex-boyfriend.

But that doesn't happen.

His eyes—green as the Irish hills, like his grand-mother always says—burn like an emerald fire as they tear through me. It's like a giant fishhook rips into my skin to cut out my heart and lay it beating on the floor in front of me, when he shakes his head softly before looking away. He never even breaks his stride as he continues to walk through the floor of the precinct leaving me behind. He's leaving me all alone.

"Did you know Priscilla was only like sixteen when they got married?" my cellmate asks me. Well, there is Evanna but I'm still not convinced that she's not a serial killer and I'm not really listening as I shake my head just as Trent had done as he walked on by.

I have to bite my lip to keep from shouting "Attica!" at Trent's retreating back. He probably wouldn't like that I and know for a fact he wouldn't think it was funny. Twenty-four hours ago, I would have thought that if I was ever behind bars clinking a metal can against the bars and shouting at the top of my lungs like I was in a movie that Trent would laugh that amazing laugh of his where he throws his head back and lets out deep belly laughs. Trent's laugh is the kind that sends shivers up your spine and makes you smile while thinking of very sexy things.

But I'm not joking and he's not laughing.

I had thought Trent and I were past the hurting each other stage. I had thought we were over the pain of hurt feelings, that the trust was there and was solid. I had thought that he loved me, that he would always have my back. I had thought that he wanted to promise me in sickness and in health for the rest of our days to love me.

I had foolishly thought Trent would never break my heart.

I had also thought I would never be wrongfully

accused of murder, even if it was the murder of the douchiest of douches who probably had it coming anyways. One who had hurt me both physically and mentally in more ways than I could ever imagine.

It turns out I could be very, very wrong . . .

CHAPTER 8

BONDED OUT BY THE BOND BABE . . . THE ORIGINAL BOND BABE

"Whitmore," the sergeant of the jail calls out in a booming voice.

"Yes!" I jump up and run to the front of the cell. "That's me."

"You've made bond," he says before punching in a code on a pin panel, issuing a series of beeps and clicks as the cell locks tumble over and the door slides open. Thank you, Jesus! I need out of this place and in a bad way.

"What about me, Big Daddy?" Evanna asks in a happy birthday, Mr. President tone of voice. "I'll be the Pricilla to your Elvis."

"No," he replies with a scowl, and the cell door slams closed behind me effectively keeping her inside.

"Make sure you come back for me!" she shouts as the officer leads me down the hallway. She's pleading and I can't help but feel sorry for her but she also still scares me a little bit. To say I hardly got any sleep last night would be an understatement. I was afraid to sleep the whole night while she slept like a baby.

"Do you know her?" the officer asks me as he leads me down the hallway.

"No," I say as my face pulls into a confused expression. I have no idea why he would want to know if I know her or not. I mean, it's not like it even matters. "I just met her in jail. Not the best place to make friends."

"Daisy is your friend," he volleys back.

"Daisy is exceptional," I tell him on a smile.

"That's true," he says after giving my words some thought. "Jones seems to be pretty taken with her."

"That does seem to be the case," I reply on a wink before inquiring, "So what did she do anyway?"

"She killed her husband and ate him," he answers in a neutral tone with a blank expression on his face. Not exactly the reaction that one would expect for a story so horrific and traumatizing. I am definitely traumatized.

"*What?*" I shout before looking around to make sure that I haven't caused another scene in here that will make Trent even more angry with me.

"So maybe don't come back for her," he suggests helpfully like he's telling me to try the rainbow roll at a new sushi place and not like I shouldn't befriend a cannibal.

"Yeah, no. I'm good," I say rushing out the words out of my mouth. "No cannibal besties for me. I will definitely stay in my own lane with that one."

"Good," he says as he leads me to a female officer

standing outside a locker room. "This is Officer Smith. She will take you to change back into your clothes and return your personal effects."

"Okay," I whisper while having flashbacks to cavity searches. This jail is not one of my most favorite places, even if I met Daisy here. I like to think she and I would have met somewhere else in town at some other time, because Daisy and I were always meant to be friends.

She leads me through the door and hands me a plastic bag with drawstring ties holding all of the clothes I was wearing when I was arrested. Unfortunately, that was my booty short jammies with a tank top and no bra. The arresting officers did let me slide my feet into a pair of Chucks, so I won't be walking out of jail barefoot, but that's also not saying too much.

I fold the scrubs they gave me and leave them on the bench. I have absolutely no desire to take any souvenirs from this experience home with me. I follow Officer Smith back through the doors from the locker room and out through the glass doors on the back of the precinct.

I let the midday sunshine warm my face. I lost track of time in the clink. When the police showed up on my front doorstep, the sun had just set and I was in for the night. As it turns out, I was more in than I had originally thought. Now, it's bright out and I can't help but wonder just how many hours I sat there and if I was sucked into an alternate universe.

One thing I know for sure is that I have to pee like a racehorse.

"Well, it's about damn time," I hear my grandmother say snappily, and I open my eyes and turn to face where her voice came from.

"Granny!" I shout, and she holds her arms out to me just like she did when I was a little girl and I fell off the retaining wall in my grandparents' backyard, causing a memory to flash before my eyes.

They had a large backyard at their old house that was separated into the lower and upper parts by a low brick retaining wall. I used to love to pretend it was a balance beam and I was an Olympic gymnast. This coordination—or lack thereof—is not something new. I have been a klutz my whole life. So I'll leave the Olympic Gold to Sophia. She's a hot mess, but she's ours, and she's way more coordinated than I am.

Anyway, I was practicing my tricks on the retaining wall one day, as little kids do, until my cartwheel got away from me and I took a tumble, scraping my leg up pretty bad. I didn't need stitches, but it had stung like a mother, and the experience had also scared the shit out of me. But my granny was there in a heartbeat.

"Granny!" I had shouted, and she had come running out of the side door to the house, the one that let out from her kitchen, with a dishtowel in her hands when she heard me.

"Shelby!" she said when she rounded the corner and saw the blood on my little leg. "Are you all right, my darling girl?"

"Uh huh," I cried as I nodded my head, but even before that I was running to her. She had held her arms open to me. As soon as I bumped into her chest, she closed them around me and I cried until she calmed me down, told me everything would be all right, and cleaned me up.

And I do the same thing now.

I run to her as she holds her arms open for me, only now I'm careful not to knock her down. She's not as strong as she was way back then, but still she's anything but fragile. I mean, I have seen her knock suspected hooker killers unconscious with her giant purple dildo named Big Thunder so she can clearly hold her own but I would hate to be the one to do anything that might cause her harm. She's precious to me.

Her arms close around me and I cry. I cry, because I was scared, and I still am. I have no idea what's happening or what I'm going to do now. I cry, because Trent and I are more than likely done for good, and I love him. Before my arrest, I was planning on spending the rest of my life with him, and now he won't even look at me and that hurts more than I could even describe.

I finally catch my breath. I hate that winded feeling you get after hysterically sobbing. I stand up and wipe my nose on the back of my hand, which—let's be real—is disgusting, but in this exact moment, I don't care. I am a sobbing, nose running, blubbering, babbling hot mess and I swipe at my face to try and clear some of it away but it is no use.

"You know what you need?" Granny asks me.

"What?" I ask on another sniffle.

"To drink your lunch," she answers. "Lets go, honey. The Dames are waiting and so is the tequila."

I follow Granny to the parking lot to find out she is driving my car and proceed to lose my fucking shit because of how many hours I had to log at the home improvement store to pay for that Jeep. But I'm also thankful and keep my mouth fucking shut, because Granny put up who knows how much money for my bond. So, I don't say anything as she beeps the locks on my key fob and climbs into the driver seat. I open the passenger door and climb in. I buckle up as quickly as possible, because Granny is hell on wheels—usually quite literally—and I don't want to accidentally fly out the window and die on the highway as she burns rubber on by just because I was unprepared for an eventuality with her behind the wheel.

"Are you out of your mind, lady?" some guy yells in the parking lot, but Granny just keeps on driving by as if she never heard him as she almost mows him and several other innocent bystanders down with an oddly placed expression on her face that can only be described as serene old lady. If I didn't know better, I would think that it was genuine but it's like the experts always say, "Don't bullshit a bullshitter" because I know for a fact that she hears them, Granny just doesn't give a shit.

She breaks the land speed record to make it to our favorite restaurant, The Runny Yolk. Alyssa, Daisy, Sophia, Marla, and her paramour, Hal, are already seated as we walk in. We take our seats at the table and settle in. There is a silence that settles over the crowd, as if no one really knows what to say. It's not like I really know what to say either. I have never been in this situation before myself. And I don't know what I need. Do I need my friends to rally around me? Do I need them to tell me that they believe me when I say I didn't do it? Definitely. Do I need a plan of action to find my way out of this mess? Absolutely.

But that's not what I get here.

Marla and Harold aren't even trying, as they make out in their corner of the booth. It's both oddly endearing and horrifying. Daisy and Alyssa pass awkward inside looks at each other from their end of the table that I cannot even begin to decipher and that really stings. When did my friends leave me behind? I could have sworn that just a two days ago, we were all laughing and drinking in the Belly Flop and thick as thieves to boot.

The waitress arrives at the table with a large, round tray loaded down with dishes and drinks as she starts passing them around. My belly grumbles at the smell of all of the fantastic breakfast foods she loads up on the table. I'm not gonna lie, jail food is not fantastic. I will not be missing it at all and I firmly hope and pray that I never have to eat it again.

"We took the liberty of ordering for you," Marla says when she breaks the vacuum seal on Hal's face.

"Thanks," I reply as I pick up my knife and fork to dig in.

Sophia takes one look at all of the plates full of runny eggs and broken yolks and jumps from her seat, saying, "Uhh . . . I just remembered that I left my curling iron on." And then she runs out the front door.

"Is she going to be okay?" I ask feeling concerned. Sophie can be a bit of a nut sometimes but never this bad. I look around the table and realize that no one else looks all that concerned. It's like I have entered the twilight zone.

"Uhh . . . sure," Granny answers my question not sounding at all sure. "I'm sure she's fine."

"Because she didn't look so good," I explain while wondering if maybe no one saw what I saw.

"Yeah . . ." Alyssa shrugs. "She'll be all right."

"Did I ever tell you about the time that I was a Bond Girl?" Granny asks me, breaking up the silence because uhh . . . no, I think I would have remembered that one.

"No." I let out a laugh.

"But it wasn't for the movies," she explains. "I was an actual Bond Girl during the war."

"Like a regular Mata Hari," I joke but when I look at Granny she is dead serious.

"No, she was a distant aunt," Granny says softly.

"Oh," I murmur, wondering what the hell kind of family I'm from and why hasn't anyone told me any of this before. This feels like something you would share during Christmas dinners when the champagne has been a little too free flowing. I mean we all know about our great-uncle's pet racoon that would pee in a trashcan on command so how come I never knew we had spy relatives? Although, in hindsight, this does explain all the years of Zombie Survival camps my dad sent me to when I was a kid and how he took me to the range with him whenever he could so that I could out shoot any of the other Army brats. Huh? How about that? It all makes sense now.

We tuck into our meals, and the large oval plate in front of me that is loaded down with eggs benedict and breakfast potatoes calls to my soul on a deeper level. I'm not really paying too much attention to anyone else around me, so I'm surprised when Daisy and Alyssa quietly push their plates away before placing cash on the table and rising from their seats.

The sound of chair legs scraping against the floor draws my attention, and I look up to see them both ready to leave. I tip my head to the side silently asking them where they are going and why they are leaving so soon but if I was expecting any explanations from them, I was wrong, because none came.

"I'm glad you're okay," Daisy says softly before the girls walk out the door.

"Where did they go?" I ask suddenly feeling unsure of myself as I sit in a nice breakfast joint in the pajamas that I was arrested in yesterday.

"They're working on a tough case," Granny explains, coming to their defense and I can't help but wonder when Granny became more in the loop with them than me? We used to be a team. How could so much have changed literally overnight.

It stings a little bit, because I just got sprung from the hoosegow and I was kind of hoping that my closest friends would be there to help me feel better and to get my feet back underneath me. It's not every day that a girl gets sent up the river for murder one, and I'm not handling it well at all. But my three besties barely stayed at all.

"It'll be all right, dear," Marla says as she pats the back of my hand in a half hearted attempt to console me but we all can see that her efforts fall a little flat. Hell, even Stevie Wonder could see that it was a dud.

"I don't know if anything will be all right ever again," I reply softly and it's true. In my heart of hearts I know that I'm not wrong. Everything is a colossal mess.

CHAPTER 9

SLUMBER PARTIES AND AMBIEN ADVENTURES

"**W**hy does my whole body hurt all over?" Granny asks, making me spit my sip of coffee all over her kitchen table. To say that her comments surprise me is an understatement.

"Uhh . . ." I fight to gather my thoughts on how to explain to my eighty-something-year-old grandmother that she popped an Ambien last night and did an entire Tracy Anderson Method video with me.

"Even my vagina hurts, and that shit hasn't been used in years!" She cackles.

At that, I have to laugh.

After the awkward brunch with everyone, where they didn't seem to care that I was scared shitless from being in jail with a woman who ate her own husband—

which I shudder just thinking about. Talk about cutting it close—I wondered if I could be wrong about my friends. It wouldn't have been the first time that I was wrong about someone that I had thought cared for me as well. After all, I had thought Bella and I were as good as sisters, that she would never betray me.

But I had been wrong then. Could I be wrong now? I hate that the seeds of doubt are playing through my mind and heart. I don't want to become that person who can't let people in. I don't want to be the person who has become so jaded that they can't trust anyone. That's not who I was before and I won't let myself become her now.

Besides, when I think about it, about all that we had been through together in the last two years, I just can't rationalize the idea that they would feel less for me than I do for them. Maybe they really are just overwhelmed with a big case. I mean, they did just open their own private investigations firm this year. Daisy and Alyssa could have landed a huge case that is zapping all their focus. But even so, I felt a little let down. Like a balloon with a pin leak. I'm just not as buoyant.

Granny and Marla pay the remainder of the check, as I have no pocketbook having just come from the pokey. I'll treat Granny to dinner later this week when I hopefully have my life figured out by then. We say our goodbyes when Marla and Harold start talking about a romantic drive up the coast in his vintage baby blue Caddy. They look so relaxed and in love and I just can't rationalize that against the part of my brain that is freaking the fuck out. Her grandson just kicked me to the curb and accused me of murder and no one seems to have a problem with it. I take a deep breath and hold it in my lungs as I try and steel myself against the hysteria that seems to be surging through my system. I feel like a pot that it about to boil over.

"Let's head to your place real quick and grab the essentials," Granny suggests and I agree with her to swing by my condo and pick up my cat, Missy, and some of our stuff so we can stay with Granny in her apartment for a few days.

"Like Missy," I add.

"I would never let you forget your precious pussy," she smirks and she says it like *puuuussssaaaaaahh*. "Then you can hunker down with me until you can get a handle on your situation." And what she really means is where my life went completely sideways.

"Thanks," I tell her honestly. "I really appreciate that."

"Of course."

We spend the rest of the drive to my condo in companionable silence.

But when I open the front door of my place, it's eerily silent. There's no fluffy kitty and her loud "where the hell have you been" cries. It's abundantly obvious that Missy isn't here. I can't help but think that something is very, very wrong. Where the hell is my cat?

Granny pulls out her phone and begins furiously texting someone—who it is, I'm not sure—while my anxiety mounts. I love my cat, and if she was let out twenty-four hours ago, my chances of finding her are dwindling. Not to mention, Missy isn't the kind of cat that would survive in the wild. She likes food from a can on a china plate, not hunting rodents. I scoop her shit four times a week, for Christ's sake. She's not going to all of a sudden shit in the woods.

Missy can't survive in the wild!

"She's fine," Granny says as she pockets her phone. "Trent has her, so you know she's living like a queen."

For a split second, I am jealous of my cat.

"Who were you talking to?" I ask but I know. In my heart of hearts, I know that my grandmother was talking to Trent.

"Let's not worry about that right now," she answers, meaning I am the only one who is persona non grata with Trent because that doesn't hurt. Not at all. "Let's just get some stuff together for you and we'll head to my place."

"I have stuff at your place," I tell her and run my hands down my face in an effort to rid myself of some of this frustration but it's no use. "So let's just go."

"Are you sure?" she asks as I look around at my living room. Everything was left exactly the way it was when the police knocked on my door last night, except for the small fact that the bridal magazines have been neatly stacked on the coffee table and my bowl of melted ice cream is now missing. I have a feeling I know who straightened up my humble abode and that it was the same person who stole my goddamn cat . . . and also my heart.

It seems the two creatures I love the most have abandoned me.

"Yeah, Granny," I answer as the truth of it all stings behind my eyes and tears threaten to fall. "I just want to go."

"All right, honey," she replies softly as she really

takes me in. "Let's go."

And we do. Granny loads me into my car after locking up my condo and drives me to her apartment in the senior citizen high rise in the Gaslamp Quarter.

"She'll be here awhile," she says to the valet kids before she hands my keys to the valet—after playing chicken with death one more time with her behind the wheel. Apparently, even the Grim Reaper doesn't want me now—before we walk through the big sliding glass doors on the front of the building.

I love my granny, but holy hell she drives like a maniac. Sadly, this is not breaking news. She has always been a maniac on the road. I have seen pictures of her behind the wheel of a big convertible with a scarf tied in her hair and huge Jackie O sunglasses on her face, and as always, she was wearing a huge smile. In every picture her love for life just sparkles. I have a feeling that her need for speed goes all the way back to her teen years, so there's no changing that at this late stage of the game. I just need to limit her time behind the wheel of my car before my insurance premiums go so high that I can't afford them anymore.

We take the elevator up to her tenth-floor apartment, and she lets us in with her key card. I have nothing but my phone and my sneakers with me, so I kick those off by the front door. Who knew getting out of the clink would be so depressing?

"Maybe you would feel better if you took a shower," Granny suggests, and I can't help but think she's right. "Besides, you stink of the clink."

"That sounds perfect," I say on a grateful smile to my grandmother. I don't know what I would do without her here. She has and always will be my lifesaver.

"I'll order a pizza while you do," she tells me.

"Order two please," I request. "I have the need to eat my feelings."

"Aw, honey. It'll be okay. You just wait and see." She winks at me before I head into the bathroom.

I'm not so sure that I share her confidence, but I nod anyway and make my way into her guest bathroom. She keeps a collection of my favorite soaps and shampoos, because I shower here regularly after yoga class.

I crack open the taps in the shower and let the room fill with steam as I strip off the rumpled pajamas I wore to jail and drop them straight into the garbage pail before I step into the shower.

I let the hot water pour down my back and close my eyes. I stand there for much longer than I should, but I just need to decompress. Unfortunately, there is no way to process being arrested for a crime you did not commit, especially when you've lived a squeaky-clean life. Well, maybe not squeaky clean, but honest and mostly law abiding at the very least.

My brain just won't shut off. I probably need to find an attorney, but I have no idea where to start. I would ask Trent if he knew someone, but he won't give me the time of day, let alone answer my calls. I know because I have tried to reach him several times today and he just sends me straight to voicemail. And the thought of him turning his back on me when I need him most has my heart clenching but also it just makes me mad.

When the hot water starts to turn cool, I wash my hair and scrub my body quickly before stepping out and wrapping myself in a thick, fluffy towel. I pad into the guest bedroom and open the dresser drawers, where I keep extra clothes. I don't feel like being pretty right now, so I pull on comfy cotton panties and a matching bra. I slide on soft yoga pants, the kind with the roll-down waist and the flared leg, and pull a tank top down over my head before making my way to the kitchen, where Granny is nowhere to be found.

"In here, honey," she calls out from the living room.

I turn the corner and move into her small living room, where pizza boxes and paper plates are stacked on her petite coffee table. But it's the giant box of wine that sits on the floor next to the table that catches my eye.

"I figured you could use a decent comfort meal," she says as she passes me a giant red plastic cup full of ice and cheap pink wine. No one drinks wine like we do: in a shit plastic cup with lots and lots of ice. It's my absolute favorite.

"You would be correct," I tell her just before I place the cup to my lips and pull in about half of the contents.

Granny stacks several pieces of pizza on a paper plate and hands it to me before picking up her own and settling back into the couch. She picks up the remote and finds a movie we both like to watch, *The Proposal*. Come to think of it, she kind of reminds me of Betty White in that movie. I have seen her cut loose after too much Boone's farm at my cousin Sky's wedding in South Dakota but that's a tragic tale for another time.

We spend the rest of the evening eating most of the pizza—mostly me—and drinking all the box of wine—also me—before Granny declares the day over and done with. She stands up from the sofa and starts to clean up the mess, but I stop her.

"You get some rest," I say softly. "I'll clean this up."

"You sure?" she asks me hesitantly. She has never been one to let someone else handle a task that she considers hers, but I like to help her out. She takes care of me, so I like to return the favor

"Of course, Granny. Thank you for everything," I say before squeezing her in a tight hug.

"Any time, my darling girl," she replies, while I start combining the leftover pizza into one box.

For as long as I can remember, she has needed a sleeping pill at night to quiet her mind down in order to get some rest. Granny has always been a high-octane kind of gal, and it's not so easy for her to slow down at night, even after an eventful day. So I'm not surprised when she pads into the kitchen and fills a glass with water before twisting the cap off the prescription bottle of her Ambien. I watch as Granny slips the little pill between her lips and chases it down with a sip of water before placing a kiss on my cheek and heading into her bedroom for the night.

I finish cleaning up the living room and switch off the television and the lights before making my way into the guest bathroom to brush my teeth and wash my face. I brace my hands on the bathroom counter and let my head hang forward, the weight of the day, of my arrest, the tatters of my life all resting heavily on my shoulders. My hazel eyes look tired, and yet my brain is whirring like an old IBM computer.

When I'm finished with my bedtime routine, I head into the guest bedroom, where a small full-size bed waits for me. Usually when I stay with my Granny, Missy is here to take up the empty space, but she's not. She's with Trent. And suddenly, I'm burning mad all over again. This is good. If I'm angry I won't feel the pain that is singing my heart. Whether it's the wine or the hurt or the trauma of it all, I don't know, but I race back into the entryway of the apartment and snatch up my phone like it's my lifeline, clutching it to my chest.

My crazy is totally showing and I don't care.

I think I've finally snapped.

I power walk with a purpose back into the guest bedroom and, real talk, this is not a huge apartment, so it doesn't take me long on a regular day. But right now, I'm fueled by my anger and frustration and copious amounts of a terrible pinot grigio, like that Ramona chick from the NYC Housewives.

I sit on the edge of the bed and slide my finger across the glass to unlock it before tapping the buttons to open my Messenger app. I select Trent's name and sally forth with zero regrets. It's like Granny always says, "YOLO."

This part is definitely the wine talking.

```
Me: What the actual fuck, Trent?

Trent: What do you want, Shelby?

Me: I want my freaking cat back, you
miserable catnapper!

Trent: I didn't steal Missy. She's
```

```
fine.

Me: She's also MY cat. Not yours.

Trent: Go to sleep, Shelby.

Me: I will in a minute. I just want-
ed to tell you that I was wrong.

Trent: What were you wrong about?

Me: You.

Trent: What about me, Shelby? I'm
tired.
```

He's *tired*? I'm fucking tired. Does he know how much sleep you get when you're plucked from middle class suburbia and dropped in fucking jail with a woman who ate her own husband? I think fucking not!

```
Me: I was wrong about you when I
said you were different. It turns
out you're just like all the others
who broke my heart.

Trent: Shelby . . .
```

The little bubbles that tell me he's typing pop up and then disappear again and again, leaving me shaking and my palms sweating. I have no earthly idea what he could possibly want to say to me at this point in our relationship.

Me: Let me go, Trent.

Trent: Shelby, don't.

Me: If you don't want me anymore, then have the decency to let me go. Give me my cat back and let me go once and for all, Trent. I can't take any more of this.

Trent: We'll talk later.

Me: No, Trent. We won't.

Trent: Goodbye, Shelby.

I don't know what came over me. I just couldn't help myself. Everything was boiling to the surface of *me* and I was overwhelmed with the various emotions that were fighting for space inside me. I didn't see if he texted anything else, because with that, I launched my phone across the small room, where it hit the wall and clattered somewhere behind a dresser or chair. I didn't know and I didn't care. Trent and I were done for good, that much was abundantly clear. I mean, he said goodbye. Goodbye is so final. It was the end, the coda, there would be no more chapters in the story of us. And that hurt so, so much.

I slip off of the side of the bed and drop to my knees. The sob that's been lodged in my chest for roughly twenty-four hours finally makes its way to the surface and I let myself give into it for a time. I had to let it out, I had to purge it from my system or else I would never be able to handle the epic shit show that is now my life and I desperately need to get a handle on things so I let it all out and cry for all the things that are out of my control, I cry for the loss of the love of a lifetime.

But then I do what my Granny taught me to. I wipe my face and stand back up.

This is the young woman my parents raised.

I am not a quitter, nor am I a victim, so I get up and get moving. I'm still too restless to lie down and go to sleep. Trent is done with me—that much is obvious. Would his trust have been nice? Of course, but I can't change other people or the way that they treat me. I can only change my reaction to them.

I am also not a murderer, so I need a plan on how to fix that situation.

Unfortunately, I can't think straight when I'm this keyed up. So I head back into the living room and switch on the television. I pull up a streaming service and begin a Tracy Anderson Method workout video that I have been dying to try for ages. She says to use canned goods as weights if you don't have any, so I go into the kitchen and grab two cans of corn.

When I walk back into the living room, Granny is standing there blinking at me in the blue light from the television with a confused expression on her face.

"What are you doing up?" she asks me.

"I can't sleep," I admit. "I texted Trent to yell at him and it left me feeling . . . I don't know . . . *restless*. So I decided to try this new Tracy Anderson Method workout video."

"Badass," Granny says. "Fire her up."

She's so chill it's a little weird. I'm not used to her in such a sedate state. But if she wants to do a workout video in the middle of the night, then let's have at it. I enjoy her company immensely and we take a yoga class together several times a week, so I think she might like it anyway. This workout series is a mix of ballet and yoga so this is right up our alley.

I start the video, which is a floor workout, and while it has a lot of yoga incorporated in it, it's anything but easy. While I don't consider myself a fitness guru, I *did* think I was in fairly good shape.

I was wrong. I was so fucking wrong.

About halfway through the video, I make a move to turn it off, but Granny isn't having it. She pops up like a jack-in-the-box. She sleeps in one of those T-shirt nightgowns and nothing else, so let me tell you, it's an educational experience on carpets and curtains for the octogenarian set. I might have to bleach my eyeballs later.

"What are you doing?" she asks me.

"Turning it off. I feel like I can sleep now," I explain. And really, there's nothing else to it. I was only trying to burn off a little of my anxiety and extra energy and I did that so I'm good now. I could probably settle down and fall asleep at least for a little while and then Granny won't feel like she has to babysit me all night. I know that she is worried about me and I love her for it, but I also don't want to be a burden on her so I'm going to let her off the hook for this workout video that appears to be a butt kicker.

"Only pussies quit halfway through!" she shouts to rival the best drill instructor. "Are you a pussy?"

"No?" I ask.

"No?" she repeats. "Are you or aren't you a pussy?"

"I'm not!" I shout feeling my spine straighten and the need to prove myself to the world course through my veins. I am not a pussy and I am going to make this girly workout of doom my bitch!

"Then let's do this motherfucker!" she hollers as she pumps her fist in the air like she's leading a band of Scottish rebels into battle.

And we did. We finished the workout video and I limped my way back to bed dragging a leg the whole time while she seemed totally fine, with a little extra pep in her step even. *Weird.*

"Why does my whole body hurt all over?" Granny asks, making me spit my sip of coffee all over her kitchen table. To say that her comments surprise me is an understatement.

"Uhh . . ." I fight to gather my thoughts on how to explain to my eighty-something-year-old grandmother that she popped an Ambien last night and did an entire Tracy Anderson Method video with me.

"Even my vagina hurts, and that shit hasn't been used in years!" She cackles.

At that, I have to laugh.

"We did an entire Tracy Anderson Method work-out video last night," I tell her while wondering if she remembers any of it at all and also how could she have forgotten?

"Since when?" Granny asks as she studies my face suspiciously. Why I don't know. It's not like I would like to her about doing a really hard work out for over an hour in the middle of the night.

"Since I was starting one when you wandered into the living room in the middle of the night," I say on a laugh.

"And I did it?" she asks, and the way she's looking at me says she thinks I am full of shit.

"Yes," I answer honestly.

"Are you sure?" she asks as she narrows her eyes making me laugh even harder.

"Yes," I repeat through a laugh. "I even tried to quit and you called me a pussy."

"Well, that does sound like me," she grudgingly admits.

"You don't remember it at all?" I ask before taking another sip of my coffee.

"No." She shrugs. "I guess it was just another adventure with Ambien."

CHAPTER 10

YOGA BRAWLS AND ROLLER SKATE SLIP-A-ROOS

"So what's on tap for today?" I ask as I sip the rest of my coffee.

"Well, it *is* Tuesday," she answers and I must have lost track of my days in the hoosegow because I am totally unprepared for it to be Tuesday of all days.

I let out a groan and shake my head vehemently. "No."

"Oh," Granny says. "Don't be such a girl."

"I am a girl," I respond on a slow blink. I have always been a girl so I'm not sure why she thinks that may have changed in the last twenty-four hours.

"I know that." She rolls her eyes in a "how can you be such an idiot" fashion. "I have the parts too . . . well, most of them anyway. I did have that hysterectomy in 1969. I just meant don't be so whiny. It doesn't become a Whitmore."

"I'm not being whiny," I whine, and she shoots me a look, the one that says *I wasn't born yesterday and I can still tan your hide if you lie to your granny*. It's a powerful look. One that scared me straight most of my childhood. The rest of the time, Granny was helping me cook up the mischief to begin with, but those are stories for another day. It also makes me admit the truth in the moment. "Okay, so maybe I'm a little whiny."

"A little?" she barks out.

"Fine! I'm a lot whiny, but can you blame me?" I practically shout at my beloved grandmother. This is not new though. Shouting is how we communicate best in our family. It's not to be mean, we're just loud and like to get our point across when we need to. "I don't think I should do anything but eat my weight in Ben & Jerry's and wait to be executed for murder one."

"You're not going to be executed," she says as she rolls her eyes. "Don't be so dramatic."

"You don't know that!" I holler. "And I'll be dramatic if I damn well want to!"

"I do know that, because I also know you didn't kill the limp-dicked little weasel to begin with," she sighs and I'm not going to lie, it feels good to have at least one person believe me. I really needed to hear that. Her words deflate my anger just a bit.

"Maybe we shouldn't speak ill of the dead," I suggest.

"Maybe he was ill before he was dead, so I reckon it's okay," she shoots back and she's not wrong either. James was a total douche but still. Propriety and all.

"Fine!" I roll my eyes.

"Fine!" she snaps back as she crosses her arms

over her chest.

We stay squared up against each other in a standoff of epic grandmother versus granddaughter proportions for quite some time until I finally blink. I was squirming long before now, so really, I held out longer than I usually do.

"Look," she says, giving in a little. It's a show of how deep in the pile of flaming dog shit my life has become for her to give me any pity at all. It is also not reassuring. "We have time. Why don't you go shower and get some rest, and then we'll get lunch before deciding if we should go to yoga class today. Which, for the record, I still think we should go to."

"And if I decide I should lay low?" I ask as I eye her looking to see if she will let me play hooky from class when I want to hide.

"Then we'll still fucking go unless you convince me it's a good idea otherwise," she says saucily with her hands on her hips. I would be impressed if I wasn't half terrified not only because, even in her eighties, my Granny still kicks ass, but also because I see so much of that reckless mouth and wild personality in myself, and that is also alarming. It's never a good view to see some of your lesser qualities staring you in the face.

"Fine," I say on a sigh. I'm giving in—*for now*—and we both know it. But, just like my granny, I can't give in completely, at least not without a parting shot. "But, for the record, I do not think I should be in public places so soon after my unfortunate incarceration."

"Duly noted," she says. "Now go shower. You still stink of the clink."

"How can I stink? I showered last night," I argue.

"You just do," she snarks. "Now go wash off the smells of bad life decisions and public urination one more time."

"Thanks," I mutter to myself before turning on my heel and heading into the guest bathroom.

I reach into the shower stall and twist open the taps. The small room fills with steam as I strip off my clothes from the night before. My nose twitches like the TV witch as I try to sniff under my arms in order to determine if I do, in fact, still stink like the clink. I don't think I smell like the jailhouse, although I do feel like a cloud of desperation is hanging low over my head right now. I have no earthly idea what I can do to help my situation resolve itself. I might just be well and truly sunk.

I step into the shower stall and let the scalding water pelt my skin. How did this even happen? How could I have gone from having everything I could ever want to having my world come crashing down around my feet?

It feels surreal.

I feel so overwhelmed and sad at this moment that there is nothing left to do but to slide to the floor of the shower and pull my knees into my chest. I let my head fall forward as the first sob bubbles up from my chest. It's quickly followed by the next and then the next. I let myself cry for the loss of the first man I think I really ever loved or loved me back, and for the loss of a man who did not love me and had hurt me, but who didn't deserve to die, nonetheless. And I also cry over the charges stacked against me. Not only am I being accused of a murder I didn't commit, but I don't even know how he died, just that it's a done deal. But the deed done by someone else's hand has irrevocably changed my life, and as of right now, it is not for the better.

When the water begins to turn cold and I have run out of tears to cry, for now anyway, I push myself up off the shower floor and scrub my body. I lather shampoo into my hands and wash my hair until the water runs clean. I scrub my face with an abrasive face wash. I know that no matter what I do I will look like Quasimodo after my impromptu sob fest in the shower.

At this point, it's kind of a lost cause.

I shut the taps off before stepping out onto the bath mat and reach for a towel. I brush the water from my skin with quick, efficient strokes before hanging the towel back onto the rack and padding naked into the guest room.

I pull on a pair of compression yoga pants in a muted floral pattern and a matching sports bra then drop a flowy pink tank drop down, letting hints of the floral bra show. I walk back into the bathroom barefooted and stop in front on the vanity. Picking up a wide-toothed comb, I yank it through the snarls in my hair before twisting it up on top of my head in a messy bun. I don't bother with makeup, instead opting to let my freckles show.

My hazel eyes glow bright green after crying. It's the one perk of letting myself feel so low. My eyelids are swollen; I look like someone with a shellfish allergy after tangling with a shrimp buffet. And yet, I can't bring myself to care. I look exactly how I feel. So I turn on my heel and head into the living room, where

Granny is sitting on the sofa under a knitted afghan. She looks so small, and I hate the stress that I cause her. I hate that she has to worry about me, and it never seems to go away, because I can't get my shit together. My life is always a mess. It doesn't usually bother me but seeing it effect my grandmother really bothers me.

"Shell?" she calls out. "Is that you?"

"Yeah, Granny," I say as I step around the corner so she can see that it is, in fact, me.

"I have a small box of Drumsticks hidden in the back of the freezer. Why don't you grab two and come on in here?" she asks me.

"Why are they hidden in the back?" I ask wondering who is going to be stealing her frozen treats. "You live alone."

"Good Lord, Hal can put away the ice cream," she says from the living room just as I pull open the freezer door. "Plus, you don't want to know what they do with it."

I can't help the shudder that rips through my spine at the thought of adventurous old people sex. I mean, I'm glad for her and all, but yeah.

"You're right. I don't wanna know," I admit to the sound of her loud cackles as the ring out from the living room.

I have to dig for a hot second, and hand to God, she must be serious about hiding her frozen goods from Marla's paramour, because they were hiding behind a giant bag of frozen spinach. I grab two, a strawberry for Granny and chocolate for me, and head back into the living room.

Only, something strange happens as I pass through

the kitchen to the living room. It's like my feet have a mind of their own. I'm not even walking anymore; I'm gliding, like an angel. *Or a demon, depending on who you ask.* It's like my feet aren't even touching the floor but I'm gliding through her apartment.

And then I steadily pitch forward as I lose my balance in slow motion.

"Oh . . . oh . . . ." I talk to myself as the ground rises up to meet my face. It's like an involuntary plank and I can't seem to stop it. I would use my hands to break my fall but I'm holding a delightfully pre-packaged ice cream cone in each hand. "This is what we're doing now."

And then I hear a loud *Pop!*

I think I've been shot.

But I haven't been shot at all. In my decent, I must have squeezed one of the drumstick pouches, because the package looks as if it exploded. I look around for it, but the ice cream cone in question appears to be missing in action.

"Shelby!" Granny calls out as she races to the kitchen. "What happened?"

"I don't know," I answer from my haphazardly sprawled position on the floor.

"I think you tripped over my roller skates," Granny says, pointing to the pristine white, lace-up death traps that have apparently been the cause of my less than graceful ice cream induced tumble to the ground.

"Roller skates?" I ask, feeling confused. "What the hell are you doing with roller skates?"

"We're roller derby gals now," Granny says in a tone that suggests this should explain everything but in reality, it explains nothing at all. I only know that I barely escaped with my life in my hands.

"Roller derby?" I shout as thoughts of angry women with blank spaces in their mouths where teeth used to be, with names like Psycho Bitch From Hell trying to run over my granny and her BFF who only has one sort of decent hip to her name. "Are you sure that's a good idea, what with Marla's hip and all?"

"Pish posh," she answers as she waves her hand in the air, dismissing all my rather reasonable concerns involving a couple of octogenarians and a roller derby. Especially one with a trick hip. "You know what the rappers say. 'YOLO.'"

"Stop with the YOLO!" I practically yell. "You're not a rapper."

"I will have you know that I would make an excellent rapper," she says rather smugly.

"Maybe a candy bar wrapper," I mumble under my breath.

And then she proceeds to prove me wrong. Where my granny is concerned, I should never doubt her ability to do anything.

"Now this is the time I tell you all about how,
My retirement village got turned all around,
And I'd like to lay it on you,
Just hang right there,
And I'll tell you how I became head bitch of Peaceful Acres.
Dun, dun, dun dun."

"Point proven," I say on a sigh.

"YOLO!" she shouts again but this time in triumph.

"Jesus," I mutter under my breath. How in the hell did I become the grownup with the voice of reason in this entire dynamic? I can barely keep myself alive, how can I be the rational one?

"Let's go to yoga class!" she cries out. "I win!"

"Fine!" I concede although I know sure that she won I just don't want to fight about it and I'm tired.

We grab our matching Reef flip-flops and yoga mats out of the coat closet by the front door and let the door click closed behind us. We make our way to the elevator bank, where I hit the button for the elevator.

The bell dings as the steel doors slide open, and we step inside before I punch the button for the basement gym, where our bi-weekly yoga class is held. I stare blankly at the doors as I let my mind wander. Anything is better than thinking about what's to come in this yoga class.

"Come on, Shelby," Granny says, breaking the silence. "It's yoga class, not a dick. You don't have to take it so hard."

I turn and stare at her. Really? Like my life could not possibly get any worse at this juncture and she's making jokes.

"Too soon since you stopped getting the good dick?" she asks as if it just dawned on her that my life is a total shit show.

"Too soon since I stopped getting the good dick," I agree just as the doors open, and we step out into the hallway outside the yoga room.

We push through the doors into the yoga room, and even though we are far from late, the place is standing room only. We make our way to the back of the room and have to walk past a sneering Ruth. Man, for all the times that mean old lady is a bitch, today is not a good one, and yet by the evil smirk on her face, I know it's coming. I just don't know how bad. Which is super unfortunate, because if I knew even a hint of what was to come, I would tuck tail and run. But I'm not that smart.

"Dudette, I did not expect you to show face here today," Harmony, our super stoner yoga instructor, announces to the room, but it's directed at me.

"Hey, Harmony." I wave awkwardly at her because there is no way I can be anything but awkward. It's me in my natural state.

Granny and I roll out our mats next to each other and kick off our flip-flops. I step onto the edge of my mat and let my toes squish in the teal foam. I close my eyes and take a deep breath to center myself, but it's no use.

"Let's start with blades of grass," Harmony says as we all raise our arms overhead and touch our palms together. I shut everything else out of my mind as I sway back and forth, loosening up my back, which was tighter than I had thought after my flight through Granny's apartment. "And now tree pose."

"See?" Granny whispers out of the side of her mouth and I know in my heart of hearts that she is about to jinx the shit out of us. "You were worried about nothing."

"Let's move into downward dog," Harmony directs us.

"Oh dear," I mutter. The downward dog is the bane of yoga for senior citizens who struggle to hold in their flatulence.

For some reason I have yet to figure out, yoga class is always scheduled right after they serve a chili buffet for lunch. If the old folks' home is unwilling to change, you would think that Harmony, after years of teaching this class—high or not—would change up the routine a little to give us all some peace of mind, but no, she does not. It would seem peaceful Harmony is a creature of habit and a lover of forward bending yoga poses that force the farts out of old people's backsides with a rocket like propulsion.

But I'm a follower, not a leader, so I take a deep breath and raise my hands overhead and then dive forward into a downward dog pose.

Faaarrrwwwaaaaaaarrrp . . .

"Dear Lord in heaven," Granny calls out.

"Oh, God, I'm having flashbacks to the Bay of Pigs!" someone shouts from the front of the room, making me bite my lip to keep from laughing out loud. The last thing I want to do is draw more attention to myself.

I then walk my hands forward into the second movement of the stretch. I take another deep breath and walk my hands backward again, pushing myself into the forward bend of the position.

Brrrrrrraaaaaarrrrrrp . . .

Jesus H. Christ. Who is that? My eyes are beginning to water with the stench.

"I'm surprised the wood floor hasn't melted from the stank," someone calls out.

"No joke," another gentleman answers. "That happened to the deck of my ship at Pearl Harbor. Because it was *on fire*!"

"Goddammit, Ruth," Granny barks out. "Quite shitting your pants already!"

"It wasn't me!" Ruth the evil bitch denies.

"Look here, you evil hag," Granny loses it. "You are the only one who can clear a room with her noxious ass-gas like that."

"I haven't crapped my pants in a long time," Ruth harrumps. "Besides, that was medically induced!"

"Sure it was, Ruth," Granny says on a put-upon sigh. "Maybe this class isn't for you."

And I would have laughed if I hadn't seen the wicked gleam in Ruth's glassy eyes.

"Well, I would much rather be an accidental pants crapper than have a murderer for a granddaughter," she sneers, and the room goes still at the same time I gasp.

"Take that back right now, you pants-crapping nut bag," Granny hollers.

"Why?" she says as she pretends to think about it as she looks skyward and tapes her index finger against her lip. "It's true."

"No it is fucking not and you know it, you miserable cow!" Granny growls at her arch nemesis.

"Granny—" I start, but they don't let me get a word in.

"Don't worry. My granddaughter Elsie will make that handsome detective a wonderful wife," she says on a laugh.

"Over my dead body," Marla growls from somewhere in the room. "Elsie is an evil cow just like her grandmother."

"It's not like a girl like Shelby could have kept her claws in him forever," Ruth adds as she innocently bats her eyes. "Elsie has a great job and a wonderful figure."

"What's that supposed to mean?" Granny asks.

"She's not fat like Shelby," Ruth answers in that tone of voice that suggests that she's trying to do me a favor while being a bitch.

My whole life, I have been curvy. Not fat, but never skinny. I've had great tits and ass since I was sixteen. But Ruth's brutal words bring back all the hurtful digs that James used to get in when he needed me to feel like I was not good enough. And it's working all over again.

"You bitch," Granny utters like a war cry just before she launches herself at Ruth, landing an epic punch to the nose. I've never seen her move like that before. I know she's in great shape. She walks every morning and we do yoga together twice a week, but damn, my Granny moves like a prize fighter.

"You broke my nose!" Ruth cries as blood gushes, but she doesn't give up the fight that easily.

"Like, old people!" Harmony shouts as she claps her hands together to emphasize her point. "This is a peaceful place. Make love not war!"

"Granny!" I yell as Ruth shoves her, but it's when the look on her face changes and she clutches her fist to her chest that I really scream.

I watch my grandmother collapse to the floor of discarded yoga mats.

"Somebody call an ambulance!" I scream as I drop to my knees beside her.

"It's on the way!" someone yells.

"Granny," I cry as I grab her hand. "Don't leave me."

"I'm too mean for that, my sweet child," she whispers before her breath stills.

CHAPTER 11

BROKEN HEARTS AND DOUBLE BYPASS

My heart is broken.

I had thought my life couldn't possibly get any worse, what with being accused of a crime I didn't commit and having my boyfriend toss me aside after said murder charges came down the line. *Oh how naïve I was.*

And then we went to yoga class. I knew, I just knew that we shouldn't have gone. I had this feeling in the pit of my stomach all morning. I had chalked it up to anxiety of the whole accused of murder mumbo jumbo but maybe it was more. Maybe I knew something like this would happen. I have a crazy great aunt in South Dakota that swears she's clairvoyant so who knows? Maybe she's not so crazy after all. If it wasn't such a dire moment, I'd remember that time she shot her husband in the ass with a shotgun shell full of rock salt because he was a cheating sonofabitch. There's even still a video of her chasing him through town on YouTube. She had rollers still in her hair and he had no pants on. But right now isn't a laughing moment.

What should have been a fun and relaxing afternoon had turned into a nightmare, with accusing stares and verbal jabs from mean old ladies. But the worst part of all, it appears my sweet, fun-loving Granny just had a heart attack right in front of my eyes.

"Don't think for one minute that this isn't your fault," Ruth says nastily in my ear as the paramedics rush in.

"Well aren't you a sight for sore eyes," my favorite paramedic, Joe, says. And he's not talking to me, he's talking to my granny.

Trent once told me that if someone was going down the tubes and fast, Joe was one of two people in San Diego County that could pull them back from the Reaper's clutches. His partner, Merry, is the other one. So I'm glad to see them both roll their gurney through the door. If Granny has any chance at all, it's because of Joe and Merry. I feel a modicum of relief at seeing them here.

Ironically, it was Joe and Merry who showed up over a year ago when James caught up to me at my old job and beat the snot out of me in the hall by the break room. It was back when I was avoiding Trent because I was afraid to be trapped in another relationship. They patched me up and Trent saved me all while joking about some fifty shades of gray BDSM power exchanges. I've been meaning to ask Merry more about that, but it's never been the right time. Like now. Fast forward to now, and I had a great relationship and he ended it, not me. *I guess I can really pick 'em.*

They each go about their tasks while volleying things back and forth to each other in low tones. Merry and Joe move so fast that I can't keep up. I do my best to stay out of their way while they work. The last thing I want is to be the cause of Granny not surviving this because I asked too many stupid questions, so I just stand back and watch and wait. I watch as they lift my grandmother and strap her to the gurney. Merry gently opens her mouth and places something under her tongue.

"Prepare to transport," Merry says as she checks something off on her clipboard and then places it at the foot of the gurney.

"Lift on three, one . . . two . . . three," Joe counts off, and then they pop up the gurney and start rolling her down the hallway at a fast clip, leaving me running to keep up with them.

Because these towers were designed with the elderly and infirm in mind, the number one elevator is larger than regulation in order for paramedics to transport when needed. Joe and Merry obviously know the drill here, because they punch the code to call the big guy down to the basement.

The elevator appears almost immediately, and I follow them while trying my best to stay out of the way.

I follow them off the elevator and to the waiting ambulance. Merry and Joe load her, and then Merry follows her on, sitting in the rear-facing seat as she begins monitoring Granny's vitals. I quickly scramble up onto the bench next to my grandmother. This is where Trent sat while they transported me before. He held my hand just like I pick up my granny's. And now he's gone from my life. I had no idea how much our lives would change in just a little over a year.

Joe closes the doors behind us before climbing into the driver seat.

The radio squawks to life, and Joe picks it up and answers. "This is Unit 40, ready to transport to Southwest ER."

"What's the status of the patient?" The radio crackles.

"Possible heart attack," Joe relays back causing my breath to still in my lungs. Shit. I was hoping I was wrong. That maybe it was anxiety or—don't know—gas or something. "Stable."

It's the stable that has me breathing again. As long as she's stable, we'll be all right. I'm not prepared to let her go yet. We're two peas in a pod, Granny and I are.

"See?" she says weakly as she pats my hand. "I'm too mean to die. I have to kill Ruth first."

I for one am caught off guard by the fact that she's awake, but I'm also concerned she's plotting murders. I have enough of that shit on my plate right now as it is.

"Maybe we should ixnay the urdermay conspiracy shit for right now," I say out of the side of my mouth.

"It's like I always say," she says softly, her eyes still closed. "There's no time like the present."

"Well, you know, I am presently out on a million dollar bond for murder," I add cheekily, hoping to sway her away from the idea of a homicide.

"Well, there is that," she agrees. "I guess it'll just have to wait for now. But mark my words, Shelby Lynn, that old Sea Hag is going down."

"Man, what kind of crazy drugs did you give her?" I ask Merry on an awkward almost guilty sounding laugh as I make the universal crazy person sign by circling my index finger next to my ear.

"Aspirin," Merry deadpans.

"Well, shit," I mutter and Merry just laughs. Here's hoping that means she's not going to report this awkward little conversation to Trent, who is chomping at the bit to send me up the river, and I cannot end up a Lifetime movie like Betty Broderick.

I didn't kill anyone. Seriously, I didn't.

The ambulance pulls into the emergency room loading zone, and Joe opens the back doors while nurses and doctors are waiting. They pull Granny out of the ambulance, and Merry and Joe are talking a mile a minute about what they found and what they did to keep her stable. At some point, I was asked what medications she takes, and I gave them as many as I could remember, but because I didn't have my purse with me, I couldn't give them the complete list.

"The waiting room is right through there." A nurse points to a set of steel double doors to me. "Someone will be out to speak with you when we know more."

"Okay," I say in a timid voice as I watch them wheel her through the doors.

"She'll be okay," Joe says as he places a strong hand on my shoulder, making me jump a little. I just nod.

"Do you want us to stay with you awhile?" Merry asks. "We can call Trent for you."

"Or not." Joe realizes that was the wrong thing to ask when my face crumples and I begin to cry again.

"I'm sorry," Merry says.

"No, don't apologize," I try to reassure her. "It's fine."

"You sure about that, doll?" Joe asks. I can tell by the look they're giving me that they don't buy the "I'm okay" line for all the tea in China.

"No, really," I say, trying to force a smile. I give up the effort when we all know it falls flat. "Trent and I aren't together anymore, so there's no need to bother him. I'm just going to call my uncle."

"I'm sure Trent would want to be here for you no matter what might have happened between you," Merry says. "We'll just give him a quick call—"

"No!" I shout just a shade more than desperately before dialing it back. "Everything is fine. Just don't call Trent. I'm fine."

"If you say so," Joe murmurs as he shoots Merry a weird look.

"I do. Just, you know, don't call him," I finish lamely.

"Sure, sure," Joe says before getting ready to leave the hospital. "We'll see you around."

"Yeah," I say sadly. "I'll see you around." But we both know I won't, because Trent is *their* friend, not me. I'm all alone.

I don't turn around to watch them leave. I just push through the big doors to the waiting room. I need to call Uncle Sal. I reach for my purse, when I realize I don't have it. *Shit!* I don't have anything with me. We left from the yoga room and all that Granny or I had down there were our yoga mats and our flip flops, which I realize that I also didn't bring as I look down at my bare feet. For worse or for better, my pocket-book with my wallet and my phone are locked up in my grandmother's apartment. They might be safe, but I also don't have them.

I let out a frustrated sigh and walk over to the information lady's desk in the middle of the room.

"Excuse me," I say politely.

"Yes?" the older woman prompts as she looks up, and the sight of her tightly curled gray hair makes my heart clench. It's the standard grandma style and it makes me think of Granny and her rollers that she winds in her hair every night. She even had them in when we did out Tracy Anderson workout. *Was that only last night?*

"I came with my grandmother in the ambulance, and it would seem I left my purse with my phone at her home," I explain. "Can I use yours to call my uncle, please?"

"Of course, dear," she says as she smiles sweetly at me. She must be one of those sock darning, cookie baking grandmas. I don't know what that's like because mine likes to party and sell giant dildos out of her pocketbook, but she seems nice. "Just dial nine before the number."

"Thank you!" I let out a sigh of relief.

She moves slightly away and picks up a checkout magazine that is advertising untold stories of the royal family. I can tell she's trying to give me as much privacy as possible, even if it's really none. I pick up the receiver and put it to my ear before dialing nine and then the number I know by heart.

"Hello?" Uncle Sal answers.

"Uncle Sal!" I practically cry. I'm so glad that he answered. "It's Shelby. I'm at Southwest Hospital with Granny."

"What's happened?" he asks, instantly alert. I hate having to call him like this but there is no way around it. Granny always says bad news is better delivered fast and to the point. There is no point beating around the bush. So I rip it off like a bandaid.

"They think she had a heart attack at yoga class," I explain.

"I'm on my way," he clips out before disconnecting.

I replace the receiver to the cradle before trying to wipe at my eyes with the backs of my hands. The nice lady passes me a box of tissues, and I take several.

"Thank you," I say softly to her.

She just nods, and I make my way over to an empty chair in the corner. There are several other families here in this waiting room, and no one looks like it's been a good day. After a while, I feel the hair on the back of my neck stand on end. It's that weird feeling like someone is watching me.

I look up, and Trent is standing in the waiting room. Clearly, Joe followed my request to not call him. He doesn't make a move to come to me; he just stands there, waiting. H he stands there with his arms folded across his massive chest, his mouth forms a flat line as he looks at me and clearly finds me lacking. In fact, the look on his face is so harsh I'm wondering if he ever found anything that he liked about me at all, and I'm not gonna lie—that stings.

I kind of want to stand up and tell him to take a

hike. I want to ask him why he's even here if he hates me so much because I just don't understand. I don't understand any of it, but just when I get the courage, Uncle Sal bustles into the waiting room.

"Honey, there you are," he says as he pulls me into his arms. "Any news?"

"Not yet," I say as I shake my head. "Last update was that she was heading into bypass surgery."

"Okay," he says with a quick nod. "So we wait. Do you want a coffee or anything? I can have someone run and get something."

"No," I say softly. "I don't think I could eat anything."

"Okay," Uncle Sal concedes. He puts his arm around my shoulders and gives me another hug. He reminds me so much of my dad. Uncle Sal is dad's younger brother, so it's nice having him here while my parents are off on another cruise, making retirement their bitch. "Honey, where are your shoes?"

I look down at my feet and, sure enough, they're bare. I keep forgetting that I don't have them on. I'm so distracted by all the things going on around me that I'm not tuned into myself at all.

"I didn't think," I answer. "I just followed Granny out the door to the ambulance and didn't bother to grab my stuff on the way out."

"It's okay," he says as he pats my shoulder. "I'm sure we can scrounge up something."

I look up to see Trent's face had gone hard when Uncle Sal mentioned my lack of footwear. Well, it's none of his business now anyway. Speaking of Uncle Sal, he is furiously texting someone on his phone. I don't know who and I don't care. I rest my head on the wall behind me and close my eyes.

I don't know how long I was asleep, but when I'm jostled awake, someone is calling, "The family of Verna Whitmore?"

"That's us!" Uncle Sal calls out as he pushes to stand.

"The surgery went very well," the doctor says. "There is no obvious cause of the heart attack, but she had one. We will keep an eye on her for a few days, and then we'll go from there. She's very weak right now, but there's no reason you can't go back and see her now, as long as you don't rile her up."

"Thank you so much, doctor," Uncle Sal says as he shakes his hand.

I look up to where Trent was before I fell asleep, but he's gone.

It's then that I realize there are fuzzy hospital socks on my feet that I know I didn't put there.

CHAPTER 12

ALL BY MYSELF

"**R**eady to go?"

By the time Uncle Sal and I were able to see with our own eyes that Granny was out of the woods, it was late into the evening. The hospital staff let us camp out for the rest of the night. I couldn't get back into Peaceful Sunset, the fancy pants high rise for the fun-loving retired persons where my Granny lives, to get the rest of my belongings. I had left everything between her apartment and the yoga studio when I rushed to follow her onto the ambulance.

"Yeah," I say as I push myself up to stand from the awful waiting room chairs. I move to stretch out my muscles, which are tight from stress and being contained in these tiny chairs for hours upon hours. "Thanks, Uncle Sal."

"Sure thing, kiddo," he says as he pulls me into a tight hug.

We check on Granny one more time. She's sleeping peacefully. The monitors beep a steady rhythm of her heart, and I can't help but feel a mixture of relief and panic. Being arrested was nothing compared to thinking I might lose my granny. I'm not ready to live without her. I would happily go off to jail if it meant I could see her every day. *Bring on the handcuffs and the strip searches!*

He leads me through the hospital in a different direction than I entered the day before. Uncle Sal had scored a primo parking spot the night before, and we don't have to hoof it through the parking garage. I'm so exhausted, both physically and emotionally, that I could kiss him, seeing his car so close. In fact, I do. I lean over and peck his cheek.

"What was that for?" he asks me with a note of surprise in his voice.

"For coming to my rescue," I answer.

"You're a good kid, Shelby."

"You're not such a bad uncle yourself." I wink.

"All right, enough of that mushy shit," he says with a soft smile just for me that does tons to calm the restless panic that has been steadily rising ever since Granny collapsed while bar brawling with her arch nemesis in geriatric yoga class. "You want me to take you home, or do you need to go back to Mom's place to get your shi . . . *stuff?*"

"I need to get my shit from Granny's place," I tell him and laugh when he shoots me a side eye that says to watch my language even though I'm twenty-five years old. "She stole my car when she bailed me out, so I have wheels there."

"I'll just help you get your stuff," he tells me.

"Okay," I say. "Thanks. I appreciate that."

We pull into the roundabout for the valet, and one of the kids working opens my door for me.

"Thank you," I tell him as I step from the car. He looks down at the fuzzy socks on my feet but doesn't comment.

"I won't be long," Uncle Sal says as he hands over his keys.

We walk side by side through the large sliding glass doors at the front of the building and sign in at the front desk but this time it feels hollow because I know that Granny isn't waiting for me on the tenth floor to gossip with or go to lunch. That though sends a pang through my heart.

"We have your belongings locked safely in the office, Miss Whitmore," the woman working the check-in desk tells me.

"Fantastic. Thank you so much," I say on a smile. "I need to get my purse and my keys from Granny's apartment. I'd be happy to take the rest up with me when I go."

"That would be lovely," she says. "And how is Mrs. Whitmore?"

"She's on the mend," Uncle Sal answers. "Thank you for asking."

"Come with me to collect your belongings," she instructs, and we follow her into an office that could basically double as a broom closet. In fact, looking at this sad, windowless room that barely fits her desk, I think it might have been a broom closet at one point in time.

A shudder rolls down my spine. I have unfortunate memories of being locked in a broom closet by a homicidal maniac on more than one occasion. First, when I was helping my granny who was convinced that a killer was taking out the old people that lived at Peaceful Sunset. The second time was when I met Alyssa. We had both been kidnapped by a serial killer who was murdering ladies of the night.

I really need to reevaluate my life.

"Please sign here," the manager says as she holds out a clipboard with an itemized list of what we left behind in yoga class. I take it in my hands and scribble my name across the signature line.

"Here, let me get that," Uncle Sal insists as he grabs our yoga mats and the tote bag with the name of the retirement center on it, holding our shoes and the key card to Granny's apartment. "Let's take this stuff upstairs."

"We are glad to hear Mrs. Whitmore will be all right," she says as we leave her office.

"Us too." Uncle Sal nods.

I palm Granny's key card as we make our way to the elevator banks and push the call button. The steel doors slide open on a ding, and Uncle Sal takes a deep breath before breaking his unusual silence.

"That lady always gives me the willies," he whispers out the side of his mouth to me.

"What?" I bark out a laugh. "Why?"

"I feel like every time she asks me about Mom she's really thinking when she can resell that apartment," he answer and I kind of wonder if he's not right about that.

"She might be," I agree.

"See?" he whisper-shouts. "It's weird!"

"It's also her job." I roll my eyes.

"It's also my job to look out for my mother," he says.

"That's true too."

The elevator stops on the tenth floor. When the doors open, we make our way down the hall to her apartment door. As we walk past each door before hers, the little wooden angels hanging by the sconce lights next to each door are flipped around. One of Granny's neighbors had the idea a few years ago to hang one of these angels outside every door, and if something happened to someone, they flip the angel around to pass the word along on the floor. These signify Granny is not in residence, and my heart clenches as I look at them.

I slide the key card in the reader on her door and unlock it. We both walk in, and Uncle Sal places our yoga gear where they go in the front closet. We are all so accustomed to Granny's ways. One day, we will have to get on without her, but today, none of us are ready.

"Do you need anything else, Shelby?" Uncle Sal asks me.

"No," I answer. "I think I'm okay. I'm just going to grab my phone out of the guest bedroom and go home."

"I can wait to walk you downstairs if you want me to."

"No," I say on a sweet smile for my favorite uncle. "I'll be fine. You go on home and get some rest."

"You sure?" he asks. "It's not bother."

"I know," I tell him on a smile. "I am totally sure. Thank you for everything."

"Of course," he says as he pulls me into a side hug. "You're my favorite niece."

"I'm your only niece." I laugh as I hug him back.

"That too," Uncle Sal agrees cheekily.

"I'll be okay. I promise," I tell him softly.

"Okay," he concedes, finally letting me go. "Call me if you need anything."

"You know I will," I agree.

"I'll be in to check on Mom this afternoon," Sal promises.

"I'll do the same," I tell him. "If you get there before me, kiss her for me.

"I will," he promises. "And I'll take you for dinner after."

"Sounds great," I agree.

And then he's gone, letting the door click softly closed behind him. I head to the spare bedroom and look for where I threw my phone when I was mad at Trent. I find it in the corner wedged behind a dresser. I pick it up, worried that I'll have a slew of messages from Trent and my friends, but when I look at the screen, it's blank. The battery is dead. Not even the little plug me in right now icon pops up on the screen when I hit the home key. It is well and truly dead.

I let out a sigh and stuff it in the side pocket of my workout pants. Really, every pair of leggings and every dress should have pockets at this juncture in our worldly technological advancements. I don't have anything else, because Granny sprung me from the pokey and the cops took me from my house. I was lucky enough to end up with my phone and my car keys, although I'm worried Granny may have hit a few things with my car when she commandeered it. And I know for a fact that she would just use a dildo to pop the dent out and not tell me about it unless I asked. I've seen her do it before!

I swipe my keys off the hook by the front door and attach them to Granny's keycard so I can get back in if I need to. I walk out the door and take the elevator down to the ground floor. I hand my ticket to the guy working valet and wait for them to bring my little Jeep Jeep around.

"Thanks," I say to the guy as he holds the door open for me.

I climb in my car and head for my condo just north of here. I don't turn on the radio, which is highly un-usual for me. I normally like to let the music match my mood, but today I feel wiped out. There is no joy to be found in my radio this morning.

I pull into my covered spot and head to my front door. When I walk inside, I instantly regret it. This place is still like a tomb. It's so quiet without my friends and family, without my cat. Which reminds me—that rat bastard still has my cat. I plug my phone in to charge so I can tell him that we won't be sharing joint custody of Missy.

It's early afternoon—well, late morning, really—but I'm starving, so I'm just going to pretend like it's time for lunch and make my way into the kitchen to fix myself a sandwich. I know it's weird, but some-times I just want a turkey and cheese sandwich at like ten o'clock in the morning. But when I do, I stop dead in my tracks. Painted on my sliding glass door in red spray paint is not a message that warms the heart. It's one that sends ice through my veins.

Keep your mouth shut or else!

Well, if that isn't just the cherry on top of my already crappy sundae.

I let out a frustrated sigh knowing exactly what this means. In the past, I would have called Trent and he would have yelled at me for sticking my nose in something that was evidently dangerous. But Trent and I are no longer on speaking terms. And when I *did* talk to him earlier, I just yelled at him to return my cat.

I could ignore the message and wipe the window, but that would be stupid—*even for me*. I need to call the police. I could call Kane, but I'm not exactly sure he's solidly in the Shelby Fan Club right now. So I do what I should, even though I don't want to. *Hey, look at me adulting and shit.* I walk back into the living room, pick up my phone from the charger, and slide my finger across the screen to unlock it before dialing.

"9-1-1, what's your emergency?" the dispatcher answers. I vaguely recognize her voice but I don't have the time to place it. I just need to get this over with. It's narrow minded of me, I know, but it's be a hell of a couple of days and I just need a nap.

"Someone left a threat on my window, and I need a police officer," I respond.

"Shelby, is that you?" the dispatcher asks. "It's Dianne."

"Hey, Dianne," I say politely, not sure what to do

in this situation.

"So you want me to page Trent for you?" she questions and I don't blame her for it. This was the standard operating procedure for when I called right up until this week. So she clearly missed the I ship Trent and Shelby newsletter informing viewers that we were no longer a thing available to ship.

"Uhh . . . no. Trent and I aren't seeing each other anymore," I answer.

"Well, that's ridiculous," she mumbles to herself and I can't help but agree with her outburst. It is ridiculous. I needed Trent and he isn't there.

"I just need a police officer to come out and take a look at the window so I can make a report," I say after letting out a heavy sigh.

"Is there anyone in the house with you?" she asks me.

And cue the freak out.

"I don't think so," I answer and I can hear my voice go up an octave as I start to panic. What if someone is in this house? "I don't know. I've only been in the kitchen."

"I'm sure it's fine," she says, and suddenly I'm not so sure. "I'll have the boys out there real soon, and don't worry. I already paged Trent for you."

"No!" I practically wail. "Un-page him."

"Can't do that. Have a good one," she chirps as she hangs up. I'm pretty sure there was nothing in the nature of that phone call that happened the way it was supposed to. Protocol much? I can't believe she paged Trent. I look to the ceiling and pray to God and all the baby angels that he doesn't fucking answer. I'm not totally sure I could handle seeing him again so soon when the wound is still so raw.

There are a lot of things I should do right now. I should go to a safe place. I should make sure the apartment is empty. I should make sure that I don't touch anything. But I don't do any of those things. Instead, I make myself a big-ass cup of coffee, because my brain needs a jolt. It's one of those yummy ones that foams like a coffee shop mocha when it brews. I look over at Trent's percolator on the counter next to my top-of-the-line Keurig, and it pangs in my heart a little bit. Enough that I consider adding bourbon to my coffee. Or picking up the whole thing and throwing it through the sliding glass door that has just been defaced by another psycho. But I know I shouldn't with the cops on the way.

Yep, that's a no on the bourbon and the property damage.

Fuck my life.

I let out a sigh and add a healthy dose of creamer before pulling up a barstool at the kitchen counter to wait for what will no doubt be an incredibly awkward encounter with the people who arrested me thirty-six hours earlier.

There's a knock at the door.

"It's me, Shelby. Open up," an all too familiar voice calls out from behind the door. *Damn it.*

I sigh and push my coffee mug away before standing up. I make my way to the door and turn the lock to open the door. Trent is standing there looking about as pissed off as a wet hen. I always wonder about that saying every time someone says it. I've never personally seen a wet hen before, so I guess I really don't know. I let out a sigh and step back to allow him to enter. His badge and gun are displayed prominently on his hips, so I know he's here in an official capacity.

Damn it, Dianne. Way to honor the sisterhood.

"What are you doing here, Trent?" I ask.

"Why didn't you call me?" he counters as he enters my humble abode.

"Would you have answered?" I toss back.

He sighs and runs a hand through his dark hair, messing it up. Not too many moons ago, I would be able to run my fingers through his thick hair, but now they just twitch by my sides at the memory of what we have lossed.

"Probably not," he admits.

"Anyway," I say, trying to redirect us away from the one-act tragedy that seems to be Shelby and Trent. "It was official and I need it documented, so I called the cops."

"I am the cops, Shelby," Trent says and I can hear his frustration over the situation ring out in his tone of voice.

"But you're not my cop. Not anymore."

Trent flinches at my words, and I kind of wish I could reel them back in my mouth like a bass line. I'm always talking first and thinking after the fact. And it always serves to get me in trouble. On a normal day, I couldn't care less, but hurting Trent was never my intention. He hurt me, yes, but I would never hurt him in retribution, and it makes my carelessness all the worse for it.

"I'm sorry," I say. "That wasn't nice and I didn't

mean it."

"I think you did," he replies softly, his face carefully blank.

"It still wasn't nice, and I apologize." He's right, I do mean that he isn't mine and I don't feel like I could call him the way that I used to when something happened. Trent and I have woven a tight life together of the last year and a half and it is going to take us some time to figure out how to untangle that and find out new normal.

"All right," he agrees softly.

"So the message is this way," I say as I motion for Trent to follow me into the kitchen.

"So the usual place?" he asks on a forced chuckle.

"Of course," I answer over my shoulder and notice him staring at my ass. I grit my teeth. I shouldn't have hurt his feelings, but I also won't feel sorry for him. Trent put us both in this awkward position, and it's not a fun one that will end in orgasms for all. "Would you expect any less?"

"Probably not—" But the words die off on his lips when he sees the message painted in red on my patio door. "Fuck!"

"So there it is," I say, waving my open hand awkwardly toward the door. "I assume Kane and the rest of the cavalry will be here soon."

"How does this always fucking happen to you?" he grounds out. Trent is clenching his teeth so hard I'm surprised his molars haven't turned to dust.

"I didn't do anything!" I shout as I wave my arms about. "And you know it. I did nothing to deserve this."

"What about when you told your ex, and I quote—"

He swishes his fingers in the air in angry finger quotes, as if that's even a thing. "—you would 'cut' him. And in a very public fashion no less."

"So what?" I cross my arms over my chest. "People say a lot of things. I just so happen to be some of those people. It doesn't mean anything."

"He turned up dead less than twenty-four hours later!" Trent roars.

"I didn't do that either!" I lean forward as I shout in his face.

"I don't know anything," Trent says quietly.

"Well, then I guess you don't know me either," I reply just as quietly. "I want a new police officer to take my report. I don't think I know you at all."

"Hidey ho, neighbors!" Kane shouts from the front door.

Saved by your ex's best friend!

"We're in the kitchen, Kane," I call out.

"This isn't over," Tent warns, his voice low enough for only me to hear but the rumble of his warning is loud and clear and send shivers down my spine.

"Oh, it's over," I whisper. "You've made that abundantly clear. Now give me back my cat and get the fuck out."

"Am I interrupting something?" Kane asks from the doorway.

"No!" I say.

"Yes!" Trent shouts.

"I can come back later," he suggests.

"That would be great," Trent says roughly.

"Don't you *fucking* dare!" I shout as I grab my kitchen tongs out of the utensils cup. "I will rip your balls off if you try it."

"Sorry, Trent," Kane says by way of apology. "Sophie really likes my balls."

"Big hockey pussy," Trent grumbles under his breath, but we both hear it. Their bromance is one for the ages. Trent and Kane are always giving each other shit and calling each other ridiculous names. At one point in time, we all felt like a family. But that was then, this is now.

"Good times, good times." Kane chuckles. "Well, what do we have here?"

"There she blows," I say as I wave to the sliding glass door, and Kane lets out a whistle.

"You sure know how to pick 'em, Shelby," Kane jokes not realizing his word choice—or maybe he does.

Trent lets out a warning growl and I sigh.

"Don't I know it," I respond to Kane cheekily.

"Let me get crime scene out here for some pictures and fingerprints and the works," Kane says before plucking his phone from his jeans pocket.

"This proves I'm innocent, right?" I ask hopefully.

"This doesn't prove anything other than the fact that you're a menace," Trent barks out.

"Argh!" I shout in frustration. "Why are you even here?"

"You know why I'm here," he growls.

"To prove me guilty of a crime I didn't commit! You could have just broken up with me if you were ready to go back to your life of ho-dom," I snap.

"You know—" he starts, but then Kane walks back in the room.

"All right, kiddies, CSI should be here soon," Kane

says as he looks up from his phone. "Shelby, why don't you tell me what happened here?"

"I came home from Granny's," I explain. "I was at my grandmother's apartment to collect my belongings. Then I came straight here. I haven't been here in a few days."

"When was the last time you were here?" Kane asks me.

"When you arrested me in the middle of a *Real Housewives* marathons," I answer dryly.

"Oops," he says. "My bad."

"It's fine." I shrug, and Kane raises an eyebrow. "Okay, it's not fine, but it is what it is. Let's just move on, unless you're here to arrest me again, and in that case, I'll pass. I could do without another cavity search by Big Bertha."

"You were released two days ago," he starts. "Where have you been?"

"I stayed with Granny at her apartment the first night, and then the hospital last night. She had a heart attack defending my honor against a mean old lady in yoga class. Her bypass surgery was yesterday. She is in recovery now. I had to go to her place to get my stuff and then I came straight here. Like I said."

"Shit, Shelby. I'm so sorry," Kane says. "Is she all right?"

"She will be," I answer softly. "But she's got a long road ahead of her.

"Good," he replies softly. "So you came home and saw this?"

"Yes," I answer Kane's question as I look back at the window with the message painted on it in bold letters.

"Anything else I should know?" Kane asks.

I pause. I know what I should do for my own sanity, but is it really fair? I don't know. I don't want to act cruelly, but I also know I can't handle being around Trent like this while worrying about Granny. I need some peace where I can find it, so I'm going to take it.

"Yes," I answer and look from Kane to Trent.

"Shelby—" Trent tries to interrupt me, I can tell he knows what I'm going to say by looking at my face.

"I don't want Trent anywhere near me or my case," I say softly.

"No," Trent growls.

"Are you sure, Shelby?" Kane asks softly.

"Yes," I answer before looking to Trent. "I can't handle being around him like this. It's not fair to me—it's not fair to either of us."

"Okay," Kane says. "I'll make it official." I just nod my head once.

"Shelby—" Trent starts.

"Let's step outside for a minute," Kane interrupts before grabbing Trent by the arm and marching him out the front door.

I sit back down on my barstool and reach for my coffee mug. I take a sip, but like the rest of my life, it's turned cold.

CHAPTER 13

"ALL BY MYSEEELF"

The crime scene unit was here *foreeever.*

Or at least that's what it seemed like. Meanwhile, Trent stood watch over the crime scene techs as they collected their evidence and marked the side of my condo with numbered evidence markers. He had a scowl on his face and his arms folded across his chest in that sexy way that means business, but I wasn't falling for it. Not this time, not ever again. Kane flitted around him like a mama bird, but it was no use. Trent and I are at an impasse.

Not to mention, they took so long I had to call Uncle Sal and cancel our plans to have dinner and visit Granny. I told him to give her a hug and a kiss for me, and then I made myself the turkey sandwich that I had wanted hours ago while I watched San Diego's finest dust my house for fingerprints.

Now that they're gone, I feel like I can finally take

a deep breath. It felt like living in a fish bowl and I was surrounded by people who know all of my worst habits and were judging me based on that inside information.

I pick up my cell phone and call Sophia. She answers on the first ring.

"Hello?"

"Hey, Sophie, it's Shelby," I say.

"Hi, Shelby. What's up?" she asks.

"Not much. I was wondering if we could get together for coffee later—" I'm cut off by the muffled sound of someone gagging.

"Uhh . . ."

"Are you okay, Sophie?" I ask.

"Yeah . . . uhh, sure. I'm fine," she says.

"So, coffee?" And then I hear more retching.

"No, I can't make it," she says as she gags again. "I think I'm sick."

"Do you want me to bring you soup or take you to the doctor?" I'm a little worried about her. She's so tiny a stiff breeze could blow her away. A bad flu could take her down for good.

"No, I'm fine," she responds. "I'll talk to you later."

"Okay," I say just before she hangs up.

That was weird. I hope she's all right.

Something is definitely off with our sweet Sophie so I decide to call Daisy and Alyssa. If anyone knows what's going on with her, it's them. If they're home, maybe I could wander on over and we could order a pizza. I slide my finger across the screen of my phone to unlock it again and dial Daisy's number.

"Hello?" she answers.

"Hey, Daisy. It's Shelby."

"Oh . . . uhh . . . hey, Shelby. What's up?" she asks awkwardly, making me feel like something really is up. I can't help but feel like there is some big secret that everyone knows but me and that feeling really sucks.

"Oh, not too much," I say. "Granny was admitted to the hospital yesterday and I could really use a friend. I was wondering if we could get together."

"Oh, man," she murmurs. "I'm sorry to hear about your granny, but hey, something just came up and I got to go. I'll holler at ya later."

And then she hangs up on me.

As Michelle Tanner would say, *"How rude."*

I have got to lay off the late night Netflix . . .

I set my phone on the kitchen counter and look around. The house seems so quiet, and I can't help but feel pretty alone. It feels like all of my friends have abandoned me since my arrest, but that can't be true, can it?

I just don't know anymore.

And I don't even have Missy to keep me company, because that rat bastard of a high-handed detective stole my damn cat! Maybe I should break into his house and steal her back. And is it really breaking in if I have a key? But I also don't even know if I should risk another arrest on my record this week.

And would you get a look at me? I'm a hardened criminal now.

What I do know is that this evening calls for pizza and a bottle of wine. I order my favorite pizza online and pop open a bottle of wine while I wait. I pour with a heavy hand and fill up the glass. Wine doesn't judge me unfairly. Wine hasn't given up on me as a friend or girlfriend. I won't try to let it solve all my problems, but for tonight, I just want to wallow a little bit so I sip my wine.

The doorbell rings and I freeze. For a minute I think maybe it could be one of the girls here to hang out with me after all. Or maybe even Trent has come to talk. I could probably be moved to forgive him if he begged.

But then a voice I do not know calls out from beyond the heavy front door.

"Pizza delivery!"

And I let out a disappointed sigh before setting my wine glass on the counter and pushing up from my barstool. I make my way into the living room and to the front door, where I take a look through the peephole and see a kid in a uniform from my favorite pizza delivery place, holding one of those hot bags in his hands.

I undo the locks on the door and pull it open.

"Pizza delivery," he says again.

"Thanks," I reply awkwardly.

"Please sign here." He hands me the receipt. I have a standing account with my local pizza place, and they just charge my card before delivery. I add a healthy tip for his troubles and hand it back to him.

"Thanks," he says as he hands me my pizza. He looks as if he wants to say something to me, but I can't tell what it is. I'm tired, I'm a little tipsy, and I need carbs and grease to heal my aching heart.

"Can I help you with anything?" I ask.

"No," he starts before obviously changing his mind. "It's just that . . . well . . . you look an awful lot like the lady on the news."

"I'm sorry?" I'm not sure what he's talking about,

and I feel my face pull into my normal look of confusion.

"It is you!" he cheers. "You're the murderer girl."

"Uhh . . ." I say for lack of an easy explanation and too much red wine.

"I knew it was you," he says as he reaches into his pocket. "Can I get a selfie with you?"

"Uhh . . ." I start to deny him, but my hands are full of large pepperoni and mushrooms with extra cheese, and as I previously mentioned, my brain is full of cabernet. So I can't stop him when he leans in really fast and snaps a bunch of pictures I know without a doubt will not be flattering and are about to be plastered all over social media.

"Well, I better go before you kill me too!" he singsongs happily on his way out the door. "I can't wait to show the guys at the gym."

I kick my door closed with more force than is necessary. I drop the pizza box on my coffee table and stomp my way back into the kitchen for my glass and the rest of the bottle, never breaking stride. How can everyone be so sure that I'm a murderer? I've never hurt a fly. Except for a few killers over the last two years, but they would have hurt me first, so they definitely don't count.

I flop down onto the sofa and fill up my glass—all the way to the top. It's going to be one of those nights. I place the half-empty bottle on the table and pick up the remote. I flip through channels, but nothing holds any appeal. Before long, I find a channel showing old *Hart to Hart* episodes. I love this show. I can't help but wish Trent loved me like Jonathon loved Jennifer. It's so unfair. I have the worst luck in love.

I really thought Trent was different, but I guess in the end, he wasn't.

I flip the lid back on the pizza box and practically dive in. I know I'm going to regret my indulgence in the morning when I feel like crap, but right now, I just can't be bothered enough to care.

I grab my phone and text Trent.

Me: Are you there?

Me: Can we talk? Please?

But there's no answer. It's total radio silence from Trent. It kind of reminds me of that Whitney Houston song that's on all the commercials now. I know it's not a sad song, but hearing her sing about just wanting someone to dance with her always makes me sad. It's kind of how I feel now, with no family or friends who can—or even worse—*want* to be around me while this murder charge hangs over my head. I'm feeling a little lonely. Okay, a lot lonely. And just like Whitney, I want to dance with somebody, preferably Trent, but he won't give me the time of day.

After awhile, Jonathon and Jennifer are off on another adventure and half my pizza is gone. All of the wine is gone, and I have moved past relaxed buzz to emotional and moody. I pull the lilac throw blanket I keep on my dove-gray sofa over my legs and lean my head back on a throw pillow that says **Y'ALL GON' MAKE ME LOSE MY MIND** stitched on the front. Granny bought it for me as a house warming present, and now I smile every time I see it. But tonight, even thinking happy thoughts of her have me feeling blue.

I bite my lip to try to keep the tears at bay, and I think I'm going to make it . . . until my thoughts drift to what Trent and my traitor of a cat, Missy, might be up to without me. Are they missing me like I'm missing them?

And then I do something I swore I would never do again. I cry myself to sleep over a man who didn't love me like I loved him.

CHAPTER 14

I SHOULDN'T HAVE COME HERE

*S*omeone's been in my house.

I know it the minute I walk in the front door. Even though my condo is dark, there is something in the air that's different. My things have been moved. The table by the front door with the bowl where I set my keys and pocketbook are gone. The old fashioned standing coat rack is on the wrong side of the door. And I can see that only one of my chucks is by the table.

I push further into my home on wooden legs and into the living room. The sofa is no longer facing the television but instead now, a window. The tv is in a corner with a blanket thrown over it. Nothing is right. Everything is all wrong.

I quietly make my way to the end table where a cordless phone sits in the cradle. It's one of those big, bulky models from the early 2000's. I pick it up and press the On button. But when I try to dial 9-1-1, I can't get the numbers right. Even though I punch the right buttons, 8-3-1 lights up on the screen. That won't get me the help I need, and I know—I just know—that I need help and I need it now. Someone bad is in my house.

"Hello?" someone answers.

"Hello, hello," I whisper into the line. "I need help."

"We don't accept crank calls here," she says.

"Wait—" I start but she is disconnecting the line before I can say anything else. Shit.

My palms are sweaty and I wipe one down the leg of my jeans before switching the hand that's holding the phone, so I can wipe off my other hand. I have always been a nervous palm sweater. My mom always called it "First Date Hand Syndrome" because if I get the tiniest bit nervous or agitated, my hands and upper lip produce sweat like it's my job. I hit the Clear button to delete the previous numbers and hit the keys for 9-1-1 again, and again, the wrong numbers appear in the window. They show 8-1-1. But again, that won't get me the police. God dammit. I need help!

"Hello?" a man answers.

"Hello," I sob into the phone. "Please, you have to help me."

"Damn kids and their phony phone calls," he mumbles. "Don't call here again."

Why doesn't anyone believe me? There's a psychotic killer in my house! Why won't anyone help me? I need help. Someone, please anyone.

"Shelll-beeee . . ." a voice calls out from somewhere in my house. "Come out, come out, wherever *you are."*

"Omigod, omigod, omigod," I whisper as my panic climbs, and I fumble with the bulky phone in my hands. "Shit!"

I press the Clear button one more time to try to get the right number. Once again, I press the buttons 9-1-1, but the numbers that light up on the screen are 9-2-1.

"Hello?" I hear someone pick up.

"Please," I cry. Oh my God, please let them help me! "You've got to believe me."

"Wrong number, dear." And then the line disconnects.

I press the Off button and then click the On button again, but this time, there is no dial tone. All I hear is a man telling me about something at work and laughing.

"And then Katie told Bells what a bitch she is," he says on a laugh. Not a crazy laugh, but a normal one. "Right there at the water cooler in front of everyone."

"Hello?" I whisper into the phone.

"Hello?" he says abruptly. "Who's there? This is a private conversation."

"Please, you have to believe me," I beg. "I need help."

"What a creep," he murmurs. "Get off this line before I call the cops."

Not if I get there first!

I'm going to the police station. Surely the police will believe me. The police stand for community, they protect and serve. They will protect me from the psycho in my house.

I grab my car keys from the hook by the door and

run to my car, not caring who sees me. I have to get out of here. I trip on my heels part way down the walk and kick them off. Barefoot is better than dead. I race to the police station and run just about every light to do so. But when I tell someone what happened, they just roll their eyes at me and walk away. The desk sergeant won't give me the time of day! What is happening here?

I see Trent heading through the room with his head buried in the open file he has in his hands, and I call out.

"Trent!" I shout. Oh, thank God! Trent is here. Trent loves me. He will believe me. I feel a sense of relief rush through my body. "Trent! I need you. You have to help me!"

"Shelby," he says on a sigh. Well, that's not the response I thought I would get from him. "What's going on?"

"There's a killer in my house," I tell him. "Everything is all wrong. Someone's moved all my stuff."

"You know that's not true," he says to me in a quiet and calm voice like someone would talk to a child.

"You have to believe me!" I shout. I feel the hysteria surging up in me. I need help! Why won't anyone believe me?

"I do, I do," he assures, but I know in my heart of hearts that Trent is only placating me. It's both frustrating and humiliating. My eyes fill with hot tears before they streak down my face.

"Let me show you," I plead as I try and dash away my tears with the backs of my hands.

"Sure, sure," he agrees. "Let's go see what's been tampered with."

"Thank God." I finally breathe a sigh of relief. Trent is going to see. He's going to see everything that's been moved and he'll see that someone has been in my house. It's finally going to be over.

I climb in my car and Trent climbs in his to follow me home. A black-and-white trails behind us in a macabre parade. I pull into my parking space and wait for Trent and the police officer to enter my condo. I wait and I listen. I hope everyone is alright. I didn't realize until this moment that now I'm worried for the safety of Trent and the other officers.

I don't hear a struggle or a gun battle. At this point, I feel like anything is possible. I tiptoe my way to the door, and when I peek through the gap, I see Trent and the officer with their heads bent close, whispering to each other. When they notice me watching, they stop talking all together.

It's then that I realize nothing has been moved. Everything is as it should be and Trent would know because he has spent a lot of time here. But it's when I look at his face that I realize that I am in so much trouble. Nothing is safe.

No one believes me.

A fist pounds on the front door.

I blink away the last ties of sleep that hold me down. I run my hand over my forehead and push back the hair that had fallen in my face while I slept on the sofa. My front door rattles on its hinges as someone pounds on the other side of it, and for a minute, I'm afraid the killer has found me again before I realize it was just a dream.

It was all a dream.

It wasn't real. It was just a dream.

I repeat the words over and over while the pounding on the door continues.

"Damn it, Shelby," Trent pleads from the other side. "I know you're in there. Open up, baby. I have to see you."

I have to shake off the hurt feelings of Trent abandoning me in both my dreams and real life before I flip back my lilac throw and drop my feet to the floor. I don't know why he is here or what's going on. I feel like everything I thought I knew was wrong and I'm spinning out of control. But I shove these thoughts to the side as I make my way to the door just as he knocks again.

"Please, baby."

The desperate tone of his voice almost drops me to my knees. As much as Trent has hurt me, I can't stand the idea of him hurt too. We're a mess really, if one were to stop and think about it. It makes me sad to think Trent and I will probably never pull ourselves together to actually be together.

I flip the deadbolt lock over and pull open the door. I take a good look at Trent. He looks about as bad as I feel. His dark hair is mussed like he's been running his hands through it. Something I know for a fact that he does when he is really stressed out or upset. He does it a lot when a case is eating away at him. His clothes are rumpled like he slept in them. His beard is thicker than his usual stubble and dark circles hang under his eyes.

He reaches out and runs the rough pad of his thumb

down the center of my cheek. I know he's tracing the path of one of my tears. My pain is for me and me alone and not for him to share anymore. I see the questions play out across his handsome face. He wants to know why I've been crying, but I'm not going to give him an explanation. I stopped sharing my life with him when he turned his back on me.

"Why are you here, Trent?" I ask softly as I lean against the doorjamb.

"Because I couldn't stay away." The words sound as if they were torn straight from his chest. Like he can't stand saying them but he can't go on without putting them out there.

Trent places his palm flat against my belly and gently shoves me backward just one step so he can brush by me and enter my condo. He closes the door, and with a soft click he sets the deadbolt in place.

"Trent?" I ask.

He takes a step toward me. I mirror it with a step back as he takes another and another until my back bumps into the solid material of the door and I let out a little "Eep."

"Tell me," he pleads as he continues to move his big body forward, crowding me in.

"W-what do you want to know?"

"Tell me that you've missed me as much as I've missed you." Trent rests his hand firmly on my hip. The pads of his fingers dig into the flesh on my body.

"Yes," I whisper honestly. His fingers flex when he hears my response and I wouldn't be surprised if there were marks left from his hold. "Maybe more."

And then he crushes his mouth down on mine.

I would like to say that in this moment, I was strong, that I held my ground against Trent and didn't fold like a lawn chair, but where he and my heart are concerned, I have no choice but to leap with my eyes closed and hope for the best. I hope he will catch me when I do, and tonight, he does.

I clutch the front of his black T-shirt in my hands and pull him to me. His body is flush against mine and I feel the hard outline of just how much he has missed me pressed against my belly. I open my mouth under the pressure of his, and Trent wastes no time as he sweeps his tongue inside.

He slides his hands up underneath my layered tank tops and brushes against my belly as he pushes my tops higher and higher over my breasts until he has to break his mouth from mine to sweep them up over my head. He lets out a growl as he cups my bare breasts in his hands.

He isn't surprised. He knew my tanks would be the only things separating me from his touch, because the first thing I do when I get home is take off my bra and my pants if I'm wearing real ones. I wear leggings more than anything else. Especially ones with fun patterns. Those are my jam. Trent knows all of this about me. He has seen me in all of my forms.

He swipes his thumbs over my nipples as he trails his lips down the side of my neck. He nips and sucks along the way down to my shoulder, and I can tell by the delicious sting that I will be covered in love bites by morning.

He leans forward and pulls my nipple into his mouth, rolling his tongue over the tip over and over again. I arch my back into him and sift my fingers through his dark hair. He lets me go. Trent raises his arms slowly to cup my face in his hands, the pads of his thumbs digging into my cheeks just a little bit.

"Tell me you want me," he pleads. There is an air of desperation in his voice that tugs at my heart and makes me feel like he feels our separation as I deeply as I have.

"I want you," I admit and the words are pulled from me like I had no choice but to give them to him. Trent has an ability to command my body and I am helpless to stop it.

"Tell me you want me as much as I want you," he says, and his hands on my face are shaking so much it almost feels like he's shaking me.

I wrap my hands around his wrists and hold tight as I look into his eyes and tell him the total truth. "Trent, I want you."

"Thank fuck."

I drop my hands from his arms and drag them down his pecs and abs. I bunch his T-shirt in my hands and push it up until I can't reach to pull it over his head, because he's so damn tall. Thankfully, he grabs the back between his shoulder blades and puts me out of my misery by tossing it to the floor.

When Trent reaches for me again, he tucks his fingers in the waistband of my leggings and shoves them down my legs with my panties all in one heap, and I quickly kick out of them. He dips his hand between my legs, and I have to bite my lip to keep quiet.

He pushes a finger inside, and I arch into him as he adds another and pumps them in and out. I rock into his hand and lean my shoulders back against the door for balance. The cool wood keeps me grounded, when I feel like I could burst into a million pieces.

I whimper when Trent slips his fingers free, but my disappointment it short lived when he grabs me by my thigh and hikes it up over his hip. He slides his hands down to grip my ass in both hands and hoists me up the door which rattles as we bump into it.

I gasp when I feel his denim-covered erection presses against my center. I wrap my arms around his neck and hold tight. Trent reaches between us and shifts my weight in his arms to rest on one knee. I hear the snick of his zipper sound in the quiet living room before I feel him at my center.

"Shell—" his whiskey rough voice sounds before he angles his body forward and pulls me down, impaling me on his cock. I feel so full this way that I need a moment to catch my breath but Trent doesn't give me a moment.

"Trent," I gasp as he slides out and slowly pushes back in.

"I need your mouth," he says, and I lean forward and touch my mouth to his, breathing his air, but I'm so far gone in the feeling of Trent all around me and in me that I can't do more than that and just hold on.

His eyes stay locked to mine and his breath fans my face as he slowly slides out and then plunges back in. Another slow slide out and then a quick thrust to bring him deep.

I dig my heels into his ass to angle my hips better to meet his thrusts. The door rattles on its hinges with each movement and I'm sure the neighbors can hear everything that's going on in the condo, but I can't be bothered to care about it or be embarrassed by it.

Trent slides a hand between us and circles my clit with his fingers, and it's all I can do to stay in the moment with the added sensation, but Trent isn't having it. He picks up his pace, pumping faster and faster as he circles my clit over and over, and before I know it, I can't hold on any longer and I let my head tip back toward the door. My climax rocks through me as my body bows backward and I dig my nails into his shoulders.

He grips my ass in both hands and drives into me with ruthlessness. He moves faster and faster, and I feel my body burn up all over again. I feel his handprints burn into the cheeks of my ass as he holds me tightly to him. It feels good to be wanted the way that Trent has always wanted me again.

And then every muscle in his body bunches tight. He's like a suppressed spring about to pop.

"Shelby," he rumbles before he tucks his face into the space between my neck and shoulder. He plants himself deep one last time before he comes, triggering my own orgasm and I follow him over the edge.

We hold each other tight. Sharing intimacies with Trent has always brought us closer. I feel my heart fill to bursting being with him again. I was wrong when I thought we were over, because he and I are obviously meant to be. I just needed to trust him to find his way back to me, and I feel sorry that I didn't, but I won't make that mistake again.

Trent lays his forehead against mine for a minute while we catch our breath. He slips free from my body before setting my feet back to the floor. I'm about to ask him to come to bed with me—I have felt really insecure these last few days, and I need to be held by him—when I see a sad look cross his face before he schools his features.

And then he rocks my world again, but not in a good way.

"I shouldn't have come here," he says with regret burning behind his every word.

"What?" I whisper. I couldn't have heard him correctly. Trent wouldn't have come here and made love to me, to feel that connection that we share one more time only to throw it back in my face. I can't believe that Trent would think that being with me was a mistake, right?

"I shouldn't have come here," he repeats the words that serve only to tear my heart out again and again.

"But I love you." I don't even know what I'm saying. I just blurt out what I'm feeling in the middle of all my confusion. Granny always says that I wear my heart on my sleeve and that has apparently not changed in all of this craziness. Unfortunately for me, it would seem that those feelings are not returned.

"I know," he says on a sad smile. That was always our thing, like Leia and Han. "But we can't be together."

Fucking *Star Wars*. Another franchise he's taken from me along with my heart.

"Get out," I whisper as he buttons up his jeans.

"Shelby—" he starts like he's going to explain to me why he gets to smash my heart all over again, but I don't let him finish. I'm done. I am so done.

"I said get out," I snap as I point to the door that we're still standing in front of, the door I had just let him fuck me up against before I knew better but I won't make that mistake again. "And I want my cat back. Tomorrow."

"Shell?" he asks as I open the door and stare out into the night. I'm not willing to look him in the face. Or maybe I can't. Either way, I know I won't.

"By noon tomorrow," I demand in a low tone.

Trent nods once and walks out of my condo and out of my life for the last time. I'll see if I can't get Daisy to pick up Missy for me tomorrow or be here to let her in when he drops her off. That is, if I can get ahold of her. I seem to be persona non grata lately and for the life of me, I can't imagine why.

I shut the door before I let myself watch Trent and his fine ass walk away. I should be used to seeing him leave by now, and yet it still stings. It reminds me of that country song about men and mascara always running. I'm sure my mascara is smeared all over my face. It's in this moment that I swear that after tonight I am never going to cry over a man again. But I will give myself tonight to get it out of my system.

I scoop up his T-shirt that is still lying on the floor and pull it over my head. I shudder when I lift the neck to my nose and smell the woodsy scent of man and sex that is inherently Trent.

And then I make my way into my bedroom and crawl under the covers where I cry myself to sleep again, this time surrounded by his scent.

I'll give him up cold turkey tomorrow.

I swear it.

Famous last words, right?

CHAPTER 15

NEW WOMAN, NEW DAY AND OTHER SUCH BULLSHIT

"Oh. My. Hell," I gasp as I look into the bathroom mirror.

It's like that scene in the new *Freaky Friday* movie when Jamie Lee Curtis realizes she's old now and not a cute teenager. I'm not old, still a sparkling twenty-five. Okay, maybe I'm not so sparkling today. But I look like hammered horse shit. It's bad. It's so, so bad.

When my alarm went off this morning, the oompah band that takes up residence in my head was pounding away in time to the beeps. I'm pretty sure that I'm dying because I don't think you are supposed to be able to feel your pulse beat in your brain. My temples thump in time with my heart.

I have never been a pretty crier. I have not ever been one of those girls who looks so beautiful and sweet after they cry who everyone wants to lay the world at their feet just to see them smile. No, I swell and puff and turn all kinds of splotchy red.

Today, my eyes are so swollen I look a little like Quasimodo. A fact I wasn't prepared to face first thing in the morning. So when I step up to the sink in my bathroom to brush my teeth and wash my face, I'm shocked to see the monster in the mirror who greets me. And I am not afraid to admit that I scared myself and I might have screamed just a little.

Honestly, it's like a bad Rhianna song.

My eyes barely crack open and the lids are so puffy. I splash cool water on my face. It helps the swelling a little bit but nothing life changing. At this point, it would take a miracle from Jesus and an act of Congress to put Humpty Dumpty back together again.

I go to brush my teeth, but when I do, I drop the cap to the toothpaste on the floor. Without thinking, I bend forward at the waist to grab it. Apparently, I was standing closer to the vanity than I thought, because one minute I'm reaching for a toothpaste cap, and the next I hear a loud *thwap* and I realize I feel very warm and fuzzy and I'm seeing stars.

I grip the cool edge of the granite counter top and carefully pull myself up to stand again and see that there is already a fairly large goose egg forming right in the middle of my forehead and it's turning a pretty disgusting shade of purple. If I thought I was looking rough before, now I look downright terrible.

I pull open my makeup drawer in an effort to conceal the nightmare that my face just became, but I'm so tired that I just stand there and look at the contents before letting out a world-weary sigh and slowly close the drawer. I also feel like I'm going to hurl. I know I drank a fair amount of wine last night, but I was fine before my collision with the counter top. Now, I want to curl up and die.

I walk into my closet and pull on a pair of panties and a sports bra before sliding another pair of leggings up my legs. I should probably throw the toucan pair I was wearing last night away. I will never be able to look at them again after last night, which is super un-fortunate, because they are my favorites.

I drop a tank top over my head and pull it down before pulling a chambray shirt up my arms. I slide my feet into my favorite pair of Chucks and head out into the day. I grab my keys and phone and drop them both into a large hobo purse and head out the door.

Usually, I like to spend some time in the morning drinking coffee and reading so that I can ease into my day, but without Missy or Trent here, I just don't want to linger. I climb in my little white Jeep and let out a heavy breath before cranking up some angry Tay-lor Swift. Her music always makes me feel even more emotional, but whatever. I'm probably about to get my period anyway. Nothing seems to be going my way. I'm not usually a gray cloud hanging over me kind of a gal, but this is too much for even me to bear. This morning, everything seems so out of my control. There is no silver lining here.

It's like my dad always says, *"In life, there are two things you can count on: death and taxes."* So I decide to head into my office at the paper. I know that death won't stop for my personal dramas. I also know that if I can distract myself, maybe the pain that is searing my chest will go away. Maybe. I hope. I mean, probably not, but it's worth a shot.

The drive from my condo to the *San Diego Metro News* usually takes roughly thirty minutes. It takes me forty-five, because I detour through the drive-thru Starbucks, grabbing a white chocolate mocha and an everything bagel that's toasted with cream cheese. I could probably use to lose five or ten pounds, but I love carbs and tacos, so that's a no from me. I just maintain my figure with senior citizen yoga two or three times a week and running from bad guys. So far, it seems to be working out alright.

Actually, I've run from a lot of bad guys in the last two years so I'm not going to feel guilty about eating this bagel anymore. Chances are it will happen again and probably soon too. Who knows? Maybe I'll be running from Big Bertha in prison so I deserve this God damn bagel and all of its glorious carbs. I also spot the Santana's Mexican Food and the salad bar across the street from the offices. I'll grab lunch on my way out in a bit. I'll probably get a salad, because it's all about balance. *Fucking balance.* I really want tacos or carne asada fries.

I finish off my bagel as I pull into the parking lot, and there are no spaces for miles. When I drive past my actual spot, I notice it's taken by a powder blue Prius, and I feel irrationally angry. Everyone knows that spot is mine. I have to park in the overflow lot out in the boonies. It's so far away from downtown that it's practically Chula Vista.

I'm glad I'm wearing my favorite sneakers as I hoof it to Timbuktu, also known as my office at the paper. I'm sweating by the time I get to the front door and more than a little out of breath when I swipe my badge. I should probably throw my Fitbit away, because it's a goddamn liar. I am so out of shape that it's not even funny. Then again, I also don't work out. These tits don't exactly like to bounce.

I walk down the hall to my department—the local events section—and plop my large purse down on top of my desk before settling into the broken-ass chair that leans a little to the right because it's missing a wheel. Sometimes, after a busy couple of weeks, I think I lean a little to one side after sitting in this chair for too many hours a day.

I boot up my geriatric computer and search my inbox, but there's nothing there. I look in all the trays on my desk and see they've been emptied out too. *Huh, that's weird.* My desk is always a little messy, and my co-workers are mostly used to it by now. Thankfully, Uncle Sal is the Editor in Chief for the *San Diego Metro News*, so I probably get away with more than I should. Speaking of, I'm just about to pick up my desk phone and call him to ask what in the hell is going on, when his voice rings out in the office.

"Shelby!" he hollers. "In my office, please."

My uncle is one of the nicest men in the world, but he does not like to be kept waiting, so I push my chair back and listen to the scraping sound that the missing wheel part makes on the hard industrial carpet. It takes a little more force than normal and I almost fall out of my chair when I give it a quick shove backwards. I'm pretty sure I have a concussion and it's affecting my balance. But *que sera sera* and all that shit. I make my way down the hall to Uncle Sal's office and knock on the door.

"Hey, Uncle Sal." I smile as I push open his office door and peek inside. "You wanted me?"

"Yeah, honey," he says quietly, and his eyes get a weird softness around them that makes me nervous. I don't like that look in his eye. In our family, if people are sweet to you that means something is really wrong, like a divorce or a flesh-eating bacteria. "Come on in and sit down."

"Okay," I say as I push the door wider and step inside.

"And shut the door." Shit, shit, shit! This is not good. I must be dying. Or my condo is being fore-closed on. Or Victoria's Secret discontinued the type of the bra that makes my boobs look fantastic.

Shit. That can't be good. I just nod and shut the door. I can't make eye contact as I round one of the small wooden chairs that sits in front of his desk and sit down. I peek up at him through my lashes and see that his face looks strained. His mouth is pulled tight into a thin line. Something is bothering him, and it's more than worrying about Granny's health, because while she's still really weak, she's doing great.

"You wanted to see me?" I repeat on a whisper.

"Yeah," he says but by the look on his face he is anything but pleased about it. The thought turns my stomach and I'm kind of regretting that venti mocha that I drank in the car.

Clearly, he's not going to just tell me outright. No, Uncle Sal doesn't want to say it at all, so I'm going to have to help him out.

"What about?" I ask. When he still doesn't say anything, I grip my hands together tightly in my lap so that I won't fidget. "Just tell me."

He sighs and runs a hand through his graying hair. "You're suspended."

"What?" I practically shout. Of all the things running through my head that he didn't want to talk to me about, this wasn't something I considered. This wasn't even on my radar at all. "I'm fired?"

"No, you're suspended with pay for now," he says as he levels me. "If you're convicted of murder, your employment here will be terminated."

"But I didn't do it!" I yell, now that my panic is in full force.

"I know that. No niece of mine is a common murderer," he growls out. Well, at least it's good to know he believes in me. It's nice that someone believes in me.

"Then why am I being suspended?" I can't help but feel a little like I am being ganged up on.

"Because your boyfriend's pretty-faced friend showed up here early this morning with all of his cop friends and a warrant to search your desk," he explains. Oh shit. I can't believe that they still think I did it! I am being threatened by a murderer and the cops still blame me for James's death. This is total bullshit!

"Was Trent with him?" I ask, even though I don't really want to know the answer. I don't want to believe he came to my house last night to dip his wick and then came here this morning with a search warrant.

"No," Uncle Sal answers and I feel like I can take a breath again.

Well, at least there's that. But if I know anything, he knew this was coming. Kane and Trent work very closely together. They've been partners for years, and the bromance has thrived almost as long. There is nothing that one knows that the other does not. They work each case very closely together.

"But . . . why?" I ask, feeling flustered and a little small and I absolutely hate that feeling. James always made me feel small and unimportant when we were together. If something had upset me then I was just being immature or dramatic. If I thought, he was cheating then I was just being insecure or delusional. I never once thought Trent would make me feel that way too.

"I can't have you here while they're searching the premises," he answers. "I have to have everything be on the up and up. Meanwhile, here is the number of the best criminal attorney in the county. She's a fucking shark and she'll make sure those clowns don't send you up the river for something you didn't do."

Uncle Sal hands me a business card and then ushers me out the door. I grab my purse from my desk and drop the card inside before sliding the thick hobo strap up my arm and heading back through the building.

"I'm sorry, honey," Uncle Sal calls as I reach for the door.

"It's okay," I say even though everything is far from okay. I still understand his reasoning and I love him, so I accept it. Then I push the door open. "I'll see you later."

And then I step out into the day and try to figure out where I go from here as I hike back to my car. Forty-seven thousand miles away. Jesus, it's so far away it might as well be on Mars. This is ridiculous.

Actually, I know where I need to go next.

I climb in my car and head straight for the hospital. I need to sit with Granny for a bit. We don't have to talk and I don't have to lay all of the heavy stuff on her, but I do need to see her and hug her. I'm so driven to see her that I don't even stop at Santana's for some carne asada fries and a drink. I just drive straight to the hospital. So that's really saying something. We all know how deep my love for tacos runs.

I pull into the hospital parking lot and find a space that's not too shabby, if I do say so myself. I shut off the engine and drop my keys in my bag as I step down from the Jeep. I take the elevator to the seventh floor where Granny is holding residence until they deem her strong enough to go home. Thankfully, she is doing better and better every day so that should come sooner rather than later.

"Yes?" she calls out when I knock on the door.

"It's me," I say as I poke my head in.

"Sweet Christ!" she shouts when she gets a good look at me. "What the hell happened to your face?"

Whoops, I had forgotten about it. It still feels a little tight and my head hurts but I am so overwhelmed with the shit storm that is swirling around me in my life that I totally forgot about the bang up job I did on my face this morning. My bad.

"Oh, I hit it on the counter this morning," I explain with a shrug.

"Are you sure?" she asks while looking me over with a shrewd eye. I can understand why she is hesitant to believe that story even though it is the truth. Granny saw me after James beat the hell out of me, not once, but several times over the last two years. It's not something you would ever forget. "No one did this to you?"

"No," I respond honestly. "There's nothing to blame here but my own carelessness. It was just an accident. You know me, I get moving too fast and it all goes to hell in a handbasket."

"That is true. Well, then get your ass in here, darling girl," she says as she waves me in. "Have a seat and take a load off."

"Thanks." I smile at her as I sit down in the world's most uncomfortable chair. Jesus, where do they find these chairs. I wonder if someone specifically designs them to be implements of torture. "I can't tell you how good it is to see you so well."

"It's good to be well," she says. "But if I have to eat one more plate of poached chicken, I will die."

"Granny, you just had a heart attack," I tell her something we all know.

"Don't I know it," she agrees. "What's your point?"

"Maybe you shouldn't be joking about dying," I suggest on a roll of my eyes.

"Whatever," she says like she's Mariah Cary with a performance rider that is a mile long with her list of demands. "But I told them if I don't get something better tonight, then I want a pack of Virginia Slims."

"But you don't even smoke," I say on a laugh.

"Correction, I haven't smoked since 1979, but I fucking will if they don't bring me something decent to eat," she yells loud enough to be heard at the nurses station.

"We know already," someone calls out from down

the hall, making Granny cackle.

"You're a good woman, Kerry," she hollers.

"So are you, Mrs. Whitmore."

"She's a good girl," Granny says. Her eyes crinkle with her smile that shows how much she really loves her nurse. "So what's up with you?"

"Oh . . . um . . . not much," I answer. I normally tell Granny everything, but she just had a heart attack. I don't want to stress her out more now when she's not fully recovered. I am not going to be the reason that she relapses because even though I know it's not true, Ruth's cruel words ring out in my mind over and over on a loop. I don't want to be the reason she is suffering. But her question also catches me off guard.

"Well, we both know that's a steaming pile of bullshit," she tells me as she crosses her arms over her chest. "Now what's the real truth?"

Dammit! She can always tell when I'm lying, and I hate that and I love it. I love that she knows me better than anyone else. I cover my face with my hands before I answer. "Granny, everything is a mess."

"Come now, it can't be that bad," she says softly. Granny has always encouraged me to share my feelings with her no matter what. In fact, when I was a teen, I confided in her what I couldn't tell anyone else. "Tell me what happened."

"Oh, you're right," I agree laying it all out there. "It's worse."

"Well, lay it on me," she says to me as she smiles. It's weaker than normal, but it's still a genuine smile from her and it does loads to ease my heart.

"I don't want to stress you out more," I admit my

fears. "What if it was my fault?"

"You didn't cause my heart attack," she tells me gently.

"I know," I admit.

"Good," she says. "Now tell me what's going on."

And I do. I tell her all about the threat that was painted on my sliding glass door and about Trent showing up. I tell her about the search warrant and being suspended from work. And even the random woman who was looking for me the other day before my life went to hell in a handbasket.

"What you need to do is to take the bull by the balls," she says excitedly and I'm not gonna lie, I am more than a little terrified by the twinkle I see in her eyes. I'm glad she's doing better and all, but that look always gets me into trouble—or a caged gold bikini that will close like a bear trap around my poor nipple—either way, it means trouble with a capital T.

"I think you mean by the horns, Granny. You take the bull by the horns." I laugh. She's not always the greatest with modern colloquialisms.

"No," she says with all seriousness. "I find men are more receptive if you grab them by the balls, the huevos, their twig and berries, the nut sack—"

"Oh my God!" I shout on a laugh as I try to stop her. "I get it! I get it!"

"I know you do." She smiles sweetly at me. "Now go find that mystery woman!"

And that is exactly what I plan to do. Among other things.

I'll just keep my fingers crossed that I don't get arrested today as that is now the ear marker of a successful day in my life.

CHAPTER 16

STORMIN' SHELBY—LIKE NORMAN, ONLY WITH BOOBS

"This is bullshit!" I shout my war cry.

"That's my girl!" Granny cheers from her hospital bed with her fist pumped high over her head like a highland chief leading his men into battle.

"Those assholes!" I growl. I cannot believe that they have turned on me like they have. It really is complete and total bullshit.

"That's right, honey. You let them have it!" She cackles and I can tell that Granny is loving every minute of this.

"His dick is not that magical!" I shout but it's clear we both know that I am full of shit at this juncture. That makes me both sad and want to laugh.

"Let's not get ahead of ourselves here," she says, stopping my man-hating tirade in its tracks. "Don't do something you can't take back. I feel like your plan of action should be to take back your power with the objective of still getting the good dick."

"Granny!" I snap as my cheeks burn with my embarrassment.

"What?" She shrugs. "There is nothing wrong with having a good man with a great cock in your life and in your bed. Plus, I want great-grandbabies."

I sigh. "He's not proven to be that great of a guy at this particular moment," I remind her.

"Ehh, semantics," she shrugs. "Now go give them a piece of your mind!"

"Oh, I will!" I shout as I stand up from my awful chair. Seriously, why is hospital furniture so terrible?

"That's my girl!" Granny claps excitedly. "Go get 'em, tiger!"

I storm out of the hospital like a soldier heading into battle. How dare those yahoos try to pin this murder on me! I would never kill a soul. I cry at every ASPCA commercial, AT&T commercial, or anything featuring a soldier, sailor, or marine during the holidays. And don't even get me started on the "Thanks, Mom" commercials during the Olympics. I bawl like a newborn baby every time. Not that I have ever had a baby, so I don't know for sure, but I'm probably right. I cry a lot. So how could someone as emotionally sensitive as me be a killer? I mean, really! Do they think a deranged killer would cry at the Pets Rescue show at Sea World? And what kind of detectives do they think they are anyways? I am a way better detective than they are.

I don't listen to the radio, but I do fume the whole entire drive to the police station. I have let too many men mistreat me over my adult life, and that bullshit ends right here and right now. It's obvious Trent and I are done with a finality befitting a Lifetime movie, so really, I don't have anything to lose . . . other than my freedom if they manage to send me to prison for a murder I didn't commit.

Granny was right. Now is the time to fight for my life. I'm like William Freaking Wallace. And man, I should really lay off those historical documentaries on the History Channel when I can't sleep at night because it is seriously effecting my train of thought.

I pull into the parking lot of the police station and into the first available parking spot. I cut the ignition and grab my purse before jumping from my Jeep like my pants are on fire. I slam the door behind me and then stomp my way across the blacktop of the parking lot.

When I get to the glass front door, I grab the handle with the force of the Hulk and fling it open. The little bells attached to it clang around like one would expect the bells on Santa's reindeer if they just did a bunch of blow in the bathroom at a rave. *Clang, clang, clangedy, clang-clang-clang!*

The desk sergeant looks up at me with a lot of anger and a little confusion playing out across his face until he recognizes me. Then his cheeks heat with an uncomfortable blush as he decides what to do with me. I let out a sigh because this is clearly my life now. Nobody knows what to do with me unless it's to slap a set of handcuffs on me and lock me in a cell with another crazed cannibal.

"Oh, hey, Shelby," he says as if he just realized I'm standing here, even though we both know he's been trying to map out his plan of action. "Detective Foyle . . . uhh . . . isn't here right now."

"I don't want to see Trent ever again," I tell him sweetly with a mean smile on my face. It's the same smile I gave Bella when I got out of the hospital and told her she could eat shit and die. That I didn't want either of them in my life ever again.

"Ohh," he mumbles, and I want to tell him to enunciate like my mean third grade teacher. "Then what can I do for you?"

"I need to talk to Kane," I say as I deliver my very polite command.

"Uh . . . umm . . . uhh . . ." he stammers.

"Now, please." I fold my arms across my chest and shoot him my meanest glare. The desk sergeant picks up the phone on his desk and dials a number. I'm assuming Kane picks up on the other end of the line by the way the sergeant answers.

"Detective Green, there's someone here for you . . . yes, sir. I know you're very busy . . . but . . . uhh . . . she's insistent and uhh . . . a little scary. Yes, sir. Really scary. It's Shelby . . ." he says after a very pregnant pause. "Okay, I'll tell her." And then he hangs up.

"Well?" I ask and I am feeling more than a little put out by the whole thing.

"Detective Green will be right out," the desk sergeant informs be before visibly shrinking back behind his desk. I have to bit my lip to keep from laughing at the absurdity of the whole thing. That this giant of a man, a decorated police officer for Christ's sake, it afraid of little old me.

I stand tall and watch the desk sergeant with sharp

eyes while I wait. I've done all but pee around the lobby to establish my dominance and it's clear that I am the victor. This poor guy didn't stand a chance. But then again, I'm a woman on the edge and it isn't even shark week yet. We could still be an episode of "Snapped" if we don't play our cards right.

Before long, Kane pushes through a door that I know from personal experience leads to the bullpen, where all of the detectives work in a cluster of desks and coffee. For a split second I feel my face fall when I wonder if Trent is back there somewhere behind the locked door with the other detectives. I wonder if he knows that I'm here or if he even cares. I just don't know how he feels anymore. I don't know anything at all.

Kane walks directly to me with a determined look on his face and his shoulders squared as he stands tall in his boots.

"Shelby?" he asks when he stops right in front of me. "What are you doing here?"

"You have to tell me," I plead, breaking the silence. I need to know what I'm stacked up against so I can fight this.

"Shell." He sighs as he pushes a hand through his mop of sandy brown hair. "You shouldn't be here."

"I didn't do it." I pause and suck in a deep breath. "Kane, you have to believe me."

"I believe what the evidence shows me," Kane says vaguely. Right now, he's worse than one of those chicks on Facebook who just posts **BROKEN HEARTED NOW, or I'LL BE OKAY. TOMORROW IS AN-OTHER DAY** and expects everyone to message them or call them and ask how they're doing with his dumb shit vague booking.

"And what is the evidence showing you?" I ask him quietly. I think we both know what the evidence is currently showing him and it's as full of shit as a Christmas goose. And that goose's name is Trent I'm a little weasel Foyle.

"That you killed James Alexander after he accosted you in the bar Friday night with his own fucking knife. A knife you bragged about keeping after you two broke up. A knife with his blood on it," he says plain as freaking day. "A knife that was found in your possession in your own condo."

That hits me like a ton of bricks. He was stabbed with the folding knife I refused to give back? But how? I refused to give it back. As far as I know, that knife is still in my possession. Or at least it was until the police found it on a warrant search. And of course, it would have James's blood on it. He was a fucking moron. Thoughts are swirling all around my head. Fortunately for me, anger wins out.

"I can explain that—" I start, but Kane won't let me finish.

"I don't want to hear your 'explanations.' They don't mean anything to me," he says firmly, effectively cutting me off. He's done listening to me. I can tell. *So much for friendship*. This is unfortunate, because I can almost guarantee that the knife found at my condo isn't the one that killed him, but it did have James's blood on it, because he was a goddamn moron.

"Then I guess I'll just have to prove you wrong," I say letting him hear my anger and frustration bubble up to the surface in my voice. If these fuckers won't help me clear my name then I am going to have to do the next best thing, I'm going to catch a fucking killer all by myself. I feel a warm glow spread through my body with my resolve finally clicking into place. Thank God I finally found my way back to my path.

"Don't do anything crazy," Kane says, shaking his head like he knows I'm going to do something crazy, probably because I am, mainly since I always *do* do something crazy and they are all just along for the ride. "Trent will lose his mind."

At the mention of Trent losing his mind over my crazy antics, I just about lose *my* mind. Trent is a lost cause, and everyone else just needs to get on board. He doesn't want me and I don't want to spend my life chasing after yet another man who doesn't want me. I want to be loved wholly and unconditionally. I don't want to have to walk on egg shells because I accidentally fall into another investigation. I want a man who thinks I hung to moon and for him I do. I want someone who believes in me even when the deck is stacked against me and never leaves me side. And I won't settle for anything less than that at this point in my life. *Look at me being a grownup and shit?*

"News flash, Kane. Trent doesn't give a shit," I say on a heavy sigh.

"That's not true," Kane says softly, looking really uncomfortable all of a sudden. He looks like he wants to say more but I just don't have it in me to hear one more person wax poetic about Trent and all of his fabulous qualities while my heart has been smashed into a billion pieces.

"Really?" I ask with so much snark and venom in my voice we should all be obliterated. "Look around, Kane. Where is he?"

Kane just stares at me with a neutral expression. What he doesn't do is agree or look around. He also does not elaborate on where Saint Trent might be in this moment.

"That's what I thought," I say softly just before I turn on my sneaker-clad heels and walk out of the station. I never once turn and look back.

If I don't get arrested again, this is likely the last time I will ever see this police station again.

That hits me like a punch in the gut.

Maybe everything would have played out differently if I had looked back and seen the pained expression on Trent's face as he stood just inside the mouth of the hallway that led to the lobby from somewhere else in the station. But then again, I always have to learn things the hard way.

CHAPTER 17

SNOOPING 101: JUST CALL ME SNOOP KITTY ...
LIKE THE RAPPER, BUT NOT.

Let's file this under "Things I Probably Shouldn't Do."

I left the police station burning with my anger. How could Kane just brush me off like that? And to accuse me of murder in the middle of the goddamn police station. All while proclaiming Trent a fucking hero. As if!

It's like they never knew me at all.

I could go back to my condo and sit and cry about another man who did me wrong like a bad country song, or I could dive in myself and see some results. At this point, there is really only one answer. The time for crying is gone; now I need to kick some ass and find a killer.

And if no one is going to help me, then I am just going to do it myself.

Or die trying. But I've shouted *"Attica!"* for the

last time.

I pull open the door to my Jeep and sit down in the driver seat, closing the door behind me. Before I buckle my seat belt and start the car, I just sit there for a moment and think.

Think, think, think, Shelby.

I tap my index finger to my bottom lip. Who would want to kill James besides me?

Only everyone.

I let out a frustrated sigh. Maybe I should go to his office and poke around a bit. He could have made a bad business deal or screwed over a colleague and who knows, someone could hate him as much as I do.

I stretch my seat belt across my body before turning the key in the ignition. I pull out of the parking lot and follow the streets over to the I-5 Northbound on ramp. James worked at a large investment firm in Encinitas. I can only hope I can get into his office but also that I can find some clues as to what really happened to him, because all I know right now is that it wasn't me but that little nugget of information does seem to be getting me very much mileage in the race against a murder conviction.

I pull into the parking lot and shut off the ignition. I take a quick peek at myself in the rearview mirror and cringe. I really wish I had stopped to take the time to slap a little concealer—or the whole tube—on my face. The bruise on my forehead is absolutely terrible. I look like a monster. Not to mention that I'm dressed in leggings with a big hole torn in the knee and a chambray shirt.

I look like I'm ready for a prison yard. In hindsight,

that is not exactly the look I should be going for right now. Whoops. This morning, I was going for comfort, tomorrow I'll have to try a little harder. We don't need to give potential jurors a guilty conviction on a silver platter just on looks alone.

I run my fingers through my long, red hair, trying to comb out some of the snarls as best I can before deciding it's a lost cause. I pull a hair tie from around the gear shift and twist my hair into a messy bun on top of my head. I grab my bag and step out of the car.

James's office is housed in a huge building made of glass windows and chrome. It always made me nervous to be here, like I would get thrown out a window for leaving a fingerprint somewhere and accidentally marring the perfection that is wealth management. James was always a stickler for perfection after all.

I push through the main glass doors and fight against the overwhelming urge to look both ways as if someone is watching me. I hit the call button for the elevator and the chrome doors immediately sweep open. What else could be expected here besides perfection? I push the button for the twelfth floor and wait. As each floor ticks by, my heart beats faster and faster in my chest.

When the elevator dings my arrival, I feel like I'm about to have my own heart attack this week. What I didn't expect was to be greeted by a friendly face. I haven't seen Mary in ages and I'm so glad to see her now. Seeing as she was James's long time secretary, I lost her in the breakup.

"Shelby!" James's secretary, Mary, says. "Oh, how I have missed seeing your face around here."

"How have you been, Mary?" I ask on a smile. She looks just as good as ever.

"Oh, same old, same old," she says before she thinks better of it. "Well, of course, before he died." The way she phrases it makes me want to laugh. Mary is no pushover. She never took James's shit for one second and for some reason, he took the shit she shoveled at him with a smile on his face. I always figured she was blackmailing him although I never found out for sure.

"How have you been holding up?" I ask softly. Mary probably really did care for him in her own way.

She waves off my concern. "Good enough."

"Can I ask you something?" I ask hesitantly. I'm unsure how she will react to my line of questioning. I'm pretty sure by her warm greeting that she doesn't blame me for James's death but that isn't something that I know for sure either.

"Sure," she replies. "You can ask me anything."

"Is there anyone who would have wanted James dead?" I ask.

"You mean besides yourself?" She laughs and I can't help but shoot her a dry smile. "Oh, I'm just kidding."

"You know?" I ask. I had been hopeful that she didn't know that I have been charged with that particular crime even though the whole thing is absolute garbage.

"Honey, it's all over the papers," she answers gently. "But don't worry. I don't think you did it. And even if you did, he probably had it coming anyways."

"That no good, lousy pile of shit," I mumble to myself while thinking that it would have been nice if the police had kept a tight lid on things instead of letting the press splatter my name all over the place, and Mary laughs again. "What?"

"I forgot how funny you are," she says. "So back to James. A lot of people would want him dead. He was about to make partner and did it on the backs of everyone else who worked here."

"Ouch." I cringe. James always did have a certain way with people and by way with people I mean he really knew how to piss them off and to do it in a way that they stayed mad for a good, long time.

"Yeah, he was not well liked here, but I'm not sure anyone would kill him," she adds. "Not even Brett, who he beat out for partner. And you know Bella thinks he shoots the moon from his ass every night."

"Yeah," I agree quietly because she did. Looking back, I should have seen that all of her excuses to get to know my boyfriend better weren't because we were such close friends. She had her eye on the prize and that prize was James. Not that he was faultless in the whole situation.

"Well, I think it's about time for me to walk this old lady bladder to the restroom. I would sure hate to have to call security if you're still here when I get back," she says meaningfully.

"Thanks, Mary," I tell her softly.

"Any time. And don't let Bella find you. That bitch is crazy," she says on a shudder as she slowly starts to stretch out her limbs which had locked up while she was sitting behind her desk.

She's not wrong there.

And with that, she pushes up from her desk and slowly walks to the restroom without looking back at me.

I don't look a gift horse in the mouth, so I make a run for James's office door just past her desk. I push open the door just a little and slip inside before softly closing it behind me. I turn around and get my first look at the office of a dead man. A man I once thought I would spend the rest of my life with. It's almost funny that his is the only ring I have ever worn but not the one I want more than anything. I don't even feel any emotion over his death—well, other than the fact that I'm scared I might get sent to prison.

His office is immaculate. But then again, James would accept nothing less than perfection. His desk is void of any loose papers or various office supplies. An expensive leather blotter rests on his desk. His sleek, silver MacBook sits closed on top.

I round the desk and open the computer. The moron doesn't even have it password protected, so I easily snoop through his files and come up empty. Even his cloud is blank.

I start pulling open the drawers of the desk and there is nothing out of the ordinary until I reach the top drawer. I feel my spine stiffen and my face go hot when I see a small velvet box sitting on top of a prenuptial agreement. Specifically, one with my name on it. It would make sense that he would have one drawn up when we were engaged, and at the time, I would have signed it happily. But this one was dated a month ago. *Oh hell no.*

With a shaking hand, I pick up the velvet box and

snap the lid open. Nestled in the soft satin pillow is the engagement ring I wore on my finger before. Before he cheated on me with my only friend and showed his true colors. Before my best friend betrayed me in more ways than the one. Before he hit me.

Before I knew what it was like to be with a good man.

And Trent is a good man.

Now more than ever, I need to prove that I am innocent. I close the ring box with a snap and tuck it back with the paperwork. I almost swallow my tongue when I see that the asshole had a weight clause added. It seems I have no right to any assets should he divorce me because I have gained weight. It also says that he has the right to weigh me every night. I think not. *That fucker.* And then I shut the drawer.

The doorknob twists and I look around. There is nowhere to hide. I'm totally fucked. So I sit calmly in the large leather chair behind James's desk and wait with my hands folded in my lap to face the music.

"You shouldn't be here," Bella says when she gains her bearings after finding me here in James's office.

"Hello to you too, Bella," I reply as I take note of her. She's thinner than ever before. So thin it looks like her bones could snap in a strong breeze. Her suit is perfection, a cream color that's immaculately pressed. And her face is covered in more makeup than the entire makeup counter at Macy's contains.

"You murdered the love of my life," she accuses, but there's something about the way she says the words that seems . . . *off.*

"I didn't do it," I tell her honestly as I look her

straight in the eye. "You have to believe me."

"I don't know what to believe," she says in a haughty tone. "You should go before I call the police."

"I'll do that," I agree as I rise from the chair and walk around the desk. "I'll see you around, Bella."

And with that, I leave James's office with no more information than I had before. I just might be sunk after all.

CHAPTER 18

YOU CAN'T BE HERE

I feel lost.

I'm not really sure where I belong. My search of James's office didn't turn up any information that I didn't already know—mainly that James was an asshole and Bella is a colossal bitch.

But still, if I didn't kill him, who did?

There is something niggling at the back of my mind and I'm just not sure what it is. I'm missing something important. I have to be, but what? I need to talk things out with someone. I need an extra set of eyes or two to tell me what I'm missing.

I need Daisy and her new P.I. partner, Alyssa.

I climb back in my car and toss my bag on the floor of the passenger seat. I buckle my seat belt and turn the key in the ignition, like that R. Kelly song. I do my best thinking to music. Music lets me express myself in ways I probably couldn't ever do verbally, so I crank up the radio. The DJs seem to know I need quality breakup music, because Sam Hunt is rolling through my little SUV. In fact, the music is so loud I don't hear Trent's ringtone play from deep within my purse on the floorboards of the car. Not that I would want to talk to him anyway.

I drive back down the I-5 to San Diego and my humble abode. I try to let my mood mellow over the forty-minute drive, but I just can't seem to settle down. I'm more anxious now than I was yesterday. It's just getting worse and worse. Although, to be fair, I have never had a pending jail sentence hanging over my head before. But this just feels like, I don't know . . . *more*.

I pull into my covered spot and put my Jeep in Park before pulling the keys from the ignition. I grab my bag from the floorboards before pushing my door open and stepping out. There's a chill in the air that wasn't here this morning. Maybe it's just me. I feel so turned around I don't know anything anymore.

I need to talk to Daisy and Alyssa. They'll know just what to do. I'm going to tell them everything that has happened. Once I explain to them how scared I am and how much I just need a friend, they will help me not matter how busy they are with their new business venture. I just know it.

I slam the car door behind me and pull my bag farther up my shoulder. It's a nervous habit I never really got rid of. My palms sweat as I grip the hobo strap in my hand while I make my way down the concrete path toward Daisy and Alyssa's ground floor condo.

When I stop in front of their door, I make myself

take a deep breath in an effort to slow my racing heart as it pounds away in my chest. I can hear voices and laughter on the other side of the door, so I know they're home.

I raise my fist and tap out three quick knocks on the door. All talking stops in an instant. You could hear a pin drop inside now, and it makes me uncomfortable. I know they're home. Or at least, I know *someone* is home.

"Oh . . . hey," Daisy says awkwardly when she answers the door. What she does not do is open it wide enough so that I can enter their home. No, my sweet friend Daisy is issuing clear "Shelby's not welcome" vibes as she blocks the doorway with her body, and I'm not gonna lie—it stings.

"Hey," I reply softly. I have to swallow against the lump in my throat. I know it might sound arrogant, but I don't understand why all my friends have abandoned me. I never moved on when they needed me. "Can we talk?"

"Umm . . ." she starts. Daisy is clearly grasping for any excuse she can come up with to not invite me in. "We're busy working on a case."

Daisy's explanation falls flat and we both know it. Of all the official police cases we've weaseled our way into, and now I can't be around when they're working? I just don't understand. Just a few months ago, I had risked everything including my relationship with Trent and my life to pose as a hooker and help her find out what happened to her missing friends.

"Oh, okay," I say. I have to bite the inside of my lip to keep the tears that are burning my eyes from falling.

"I get it."

Movement over Daisy's shoulder catches my eye, and I see Jones and another man with a badge inside the apartment. Jones has been Daisy's sweetheart for a while, but this new guy I don't know. There are empty plates and beer bottles around the dining table where Alyssa sits with the two men.

Clearly, there was a double date and I'm intruding. My heart pangs with jealousy when I realize Daisy and Alyssa have each other and apparently don't need me anymore. Sophie never answers her phone anymore, and I probably won't hear from her again, since I had it out with Kane in the lobby of the police department. I'm new to the friend business, but I'm guessing friendships don't usually survive one friend yelling at the other one's husband like a crazy person.

Jones slides his chair back and unfolds his large-framed body as he stands up and makes his way over to the door where Daisy stands in front of me. There is an unhappy look on his face that I have never seen before and one I definitely never want to see again. It's... intimidating.

"You can't be here," he says, and I jump a little at his deep, booming voice.

"Oh, okay," I whisper. "I get it."

"Shelby—" Daisy starts as I turn away.

"No, it's okay," I say as I wave my arm in the air to let them know there are no hard feelings. What I *do not do* is turn around, because now the tears I tried so hard to stop are sliding down my cheeks. "I understand. I'll see you around."

I start walking, but I don't want to go home. I'm

not ready to be alone yet. I walk past my own place and down to the mailboxes. The sun is setting in gorgeous shades of orange sherbet and fuchsia with just the tiniest bits of blue. My mom calls them Lovers' Sunsets. She says they're meant to be shared with a lover. I miss her. I miss both of my parents and I wish they were here with me right now. But at the same time, I'm glad they are getting to live their dreams of travelling the world. They're on the coast of Italy now and last I heard the food was fantastic and my mom though the Swiss Guard were hot which was a little nugget of information that my dad did not find at all funny.

I slide my bag down my arm and dig through it for my keys. How is it that they always seem to end up at the very bottom of my purse under all the crap, like Target receipts from six months ago and a half eaten bag of old jelly beans. I'm pretty sure those are still good though. My fingers finally brush the metal keyring. I loop my finger through the ring and pluck them from the depths of my bag. I slide each key out of the way like an old school jailor until I get to my tiny mailbox key. I grab the whole wad of envelopes and mailer coupons out of the mailbox and shut the door.

When I turn, my pervy neighbor Steve is standing at the entrance to the mailbox platform. I wonder what he's up to tonight. Maybe we can hang out. He's always super nice to me even if he is slightly lecherous in a totally non-threatening way. I bet we could grab a pizza and visit for a while. I have a sneaky suspicion that he might have a great sense of humor or a dry wit and I want to tap into that.

"Hi, Steve! I didn't see you there." I smile brightly

at him.

"Oh . . . uhh . . . hey, Shelby," he stammers looking over my shoulder and not quite meeting my eyes. Steve is shuffling his feet in a nervous way and for the first time in a long time he looks really uncomfortable around me and not in his usual he's just nervous around a girl that he thinks is pretty kind of a way.

"Want to watch a movie and order some takeout?" I ask him. I can hear the excitement and the hopefulness in my voice and I'm not gonna lie, I sound a little desperate. "I could do pizza or Chinese."

"Oh . . . umm . . . I can't. I'm busy. Washing my cat," Steve says as he looks not at my face but my right ear. A not good feeling sinks into the pit of my stomach. He's lying and we both know it.

"You don't have a cat," I tell him as I narrow my eyes on him. Why is he lying to me now? I don't like this at all. But his answer hits me like a wrecking ball.

"Okay," he agrees quickly and I know that whatever comes out of his mouth next is going to level me. And I'm right. I'm starting to really hate being right. "I don't hang out with killers."

"Oh, all right." I hear my breath catch in my throat. I'm going to cry—again—and I really hate crying. I just want to feel okay again. I hate feeling this hurt, I hate feeling so alone. But I hate a feeling it's going to be a long time before I feel any sense of normal again at all.

I did not see that one coming. I mean, it's illegal to peep into windows, so I figured he'd be decent about the whole accused of murder business. I guess not. And that hurts too. Lately, everywhere I turn has someone walking away from me. And it really fucking hurts.

CHAPTER 19

NOT AGAIN

By the time I walk back to my condo from the mail-boxes, I'm flat out bawling.

Even Pervy Steve doesn't want to hang out with me. Am I really that bad? I think I'm a pretty nice gal, but I guess . . . what do I even know anyways?

"Come on, come on," I chant as I finally get the door open in spite of my blurry vision. I'm sniffling as I fumble with my house key in the deadbolt on the front door, making it difficult to see the lock.

I dump my bag and the mail down on the cute little table I use as a catch-all by the front door and try to wipe my eyes with the back of my hands. I plop my keys down on top of it all before padding across the living room to flop down on the sofa. Nobody wants me anymore!

"Damn it," I grumble as my belly growls and I push myself back up off of the sofa.

I stomp as I make my way back to the entryway table and pluck my phone from my purse. I kick my sneakers off by the front door as I call into my favorite pizza place.

"Pizza House, this is Juan. Can I take your order?" someone answers the phone at my favorite pizza place. I feel like Juan is the only one who will understand me and appreciate me at this juncture in my life.

"I-I-I need a large pizza with pepperoni and mush-rooms," I sob into the phone. "And a side of less f-f-f-feelings."

"Uhh . . ." the kid who answered the phone says awkwardly. "I don't think we can give you less feel-ings. Will . . . uhh . . . will that be okay?"

Apparently, he doesn't understand me. That sucks.

But he's sweet. He'll probably grow up and be a great human being and not ever break any hearts. If I was ever going to have a kid, I would want them to end up with someone as thoughtful and considerate of their feelings as Juan here is. I also don't know why I'm thinking of him as a kid because I'm probably five years older than him tops. This drama in my life with Trent and all of my friends, not to mention the murder rap I have to find my way out of and my Granny's pre-carious health situation have aged me greatly. I'm an old woman now. I wouldn't be at all surprised if my hair was gray. God, I hope my hair isn't gray. I love my red hair. Shit. I'm really losing it and I'm just trying to order pizza. The thought makes me start crying again.

"I-I-It's okay," I sniffle. "I'm just going to eat them."

"So that'll be one large pizza with pepperoni and

mushroom, correct?" he asks without missing a beat.

"Yeah," I answer and wipe my nose on the back of my hand. It's not my finer moment but whatever. It is what it is.

"To the address linked to this phone number?" he asks me all business now and clearly trying to get the crazy lady off of the phone.

"Yes," I whisper. Trent always ordered the pizza at his house. Trent and I are never going to order pizza together again and the thought of not doing something so mundane with him ever again makes my heart bleed.

"It'll be $17.85," Juan tells me, and I give him my credit card number. "Your pizza should be there in about twenty minutes."

"Thanks, Juan," I say through a sniffle. I'm just about to hang up, when Juan rocks my world.

"He doesn't deserve you," he murmurs. "If he makes you cry like this, then he isn't worth it."

"Thanks, Juan."

"Have a good night, Miss Shelby."

I end the call with Juan and bounce around my condo for a while. I crank up my favorite breakup playlist and dance around. Even though Juan is right, I still cry. I have to get it out. I'm a very emotional person, and I have to be able to express those emotions or else I will explode into a big old pile of Shelby shit sandwich.

I pass the stack of mail I had brought in with me and stop to pick it up. I carry it into the kitchen to deal with it, because I don't like clutter or things lying around like that. I'm naturally a slob, so I have to be cognizant of the mess I make or else this place turns into a nightmare real fast. My mother is a neat freak and would die if that happened. Plus, I'm in bad breakup mode, so anything is possible right now.

I set the stack on the kitchen island and begin flipping through it. I set the envelopes aside and throw the mailer coupons into the trash. I am definitely not organized enough to sort and clip coupons. I flip through the envelopes once more and sort them *bills . . . bills . . . bills . . .* and I'm singing the Destiny's Child song while I flip through my mail because my musical stylings are literally all I have going for me right now. And then a handwritten notecard. With no stamp or return address or otherwise on the envelope.

My spidey senses are tingling.

I pick up the envelope and slide my fingernail under the flap to rip it open. Inside, the notecard is written in perfect penmanship.

This is your last warning.
Keep your fat ass out of my business or you are next!

I let out a sigh. "Oh, not again."

It's like Granny always says, "If it walks like a duck and it quacks like a duck, it's probably a threat mailed to you by the killer." And it would appear that her words of wisdom still ring true.

Shit. Shit. Shit!

What am I going to do? I can't call Trent. I can't call Daisy or Alyssa. Sophie is so sick she's hurling every time I try to talk to her on the phone, and now her husband probably hates me, so I can't call her either.

So I do what any self-respecting woman would

do. I cranked up the volume on my breakup music and dance and cry until my pizza shows up.

"Tuuurn arooound . . ."

I sing along to one of my favorite songs at the top of my lungs as tears stream down my face. In the last hour, I have decided it is the new anthem for my life. After all, once I was in love, and now my life is a mess.

Seriously, why don't they write music like this anymore? Also, this may be the dehydration from crying so much talking.

I decide to take a mental and physical break from my bad breakup dance party and pause the music. I head into the kitchen and grab a bottle of water from the fridge. I crack the cap and chug it like it's a fraternity party.

I feel backed into a corner. I feel all alone. I can't call Trent. I can't call Kane. Or even Daisy and Alyssa. I hate to burden Granny with more of my problems, but I just have to hear her voice. And with my parents out of the country, she's the only one I can turn to.

I know for a fact Uncle Sal brought her a bunch of her belongings today to make her hospital stay more comfortable. Things like pajamas, her favorite magazines with crossword puzzles in the back, and her cell phone.

I pick my own phone back up and slide my finger across the screen to unlock it. I find her number at the top of my favorites list and call. She answers on the first ring, and I'm not surprised, because she's a night owl just like me.

"Hello?"

"Hey, Granny," I say, and I hear my lip quiver as I talk. "It's me."

"Oh, honey. What's wrong?" Granny always knows me better than I know myself. I don't hide anything from her. I never could, so instead, I tell her everything.

"Everything," I answer. "Kane thinks I killed James, because they found his knife here at my house with traces of his blood on it."

"Because James is a moron," she harrumphs. "Remember when that asshole was dicking around with it and stabbed his foot by accident?"

"I do," I answer her.

"Well, did you tell Kane that? That it's old blood?" she asks, and I can tell she's getting mad on my behalf.

"I tried, but he wouldn't listen to me," I explain. "They think that is the murder weapon."

"Well, clearly, it's not," she says calmly. "The idiot must have had two."

"It's possible," I murmur, thinking about the knife James had wanted back so badly. "It was part of a set from his grandfather's estate. At least I *think* I remember him saying at one point it was part of a set. But honestly, I just didn't care. I was angry and wanted him to know what it felt like to want something you can't have." I'm regretting my short bout of pettiness. It's not a good look on me and it clearly landed my ass in more hot water than I bargained for.

"As anyone would do," she drolls. She pauses for a minute to collect her thoughts before speaking again. "I feel like there's something else weighing on your mind."

I sigh. "There is."

"And that would be?" she asks. "Child, we don't have all day here."

"I got another threat in the mail to stop looking into James's death," I admit. I really didn't want to say it out loud. It's like if I don't admit it, it's not really happening but that is the not the mature, grownup way to handle things here. And it could also get me killed. Although if I'm dead I can't be sent to prison for a crime I didn't commit, so there is that . . .

"Tell me about it." She waits quietly while I explain.

"It had no stamp or addresses to me or from anyone," I tell her. "It's like it was just slipped into my mailbox with the rest of my mail."

"What did it say?" she asks.

"Something about my keeping my fat ass out of their business or else, mumbo jumbo," I tell her while I roll my eyes. "Honestly, now that the shock has worn off, it's stupid, really."

"I wouldn't discount it as stupid, honey," Granny says cautiously which is not usually her modus operandi. "I think you should report it."

"To who?" I ask. "I can't call Trent or Kane. And every time I call the police, they show up anyway. And always angry and blaming me for what happened to James. It's all getting really fucking frustrating."

"I know, honey," she says softly. "But I really think you have to do something about this. What about Daisy and Alyssa?"

"They are on a double date with a couple cops who threw me out when I tried to go talk to them after a really bad day," I say pushing out a frustrated breath.

"Really?" she prompts. "That doesn't seem right."

"I know!" I shout because I can't believe it either. It feels good to hear Granny echo my thoughts and feelings on the matter.

"But I think you need to tell them about the knife," she says.

She continues talking, but there's something about the note that is pulling at the back of my mind and I just can't seem to put my finger on it. All I know is, I have to find another knife to prove it wasn't me.

This might be my last chance.

"Granny," I tell her. "I have to go. I have an idea."

"What idea?" she practically shouts, and then says to someone else, "Oh shut up, you cow. Half the people in here are deaf anyway. I'll shout if I want to."

"Granny—" I start, but she won't let me finish.

"Where are you going?" she asks me.

"I have to go to James's house," I explain. "I think I'll find the answers I need there."

"No," she says quickly. "Let's call Trent anyway."

"No," I reply sadly. "He won't believe me."

"I think you should give him a chance, honey," she murmurs softly. "I don't think you're thinking this through."

"Trent has had all the chances," I tell her. "Besides, this princess always saves herself anyway."

"You do realize when this particular princess usually saves herself, she has a team of crazy old ladies, a couple hookers—"

"Retired hookers," I interrupt her.

"—retired hookers, and a figure skater, all wielding

dildos," she reminds helpfully and I smile sadly thinking about the good old days when we were all a team. But that was then, this is now, and I'm all alone.

"Don't forget Miss Marla's desert eagle," I add.

"Who could forget the eagle?" Granny agrees with a wistful tone of voice. "That is one badass piece of Israeli machinery."

"True," I concede. I needed the smile she puts on my face. Granny always calms me, but now I know exactly what I need to do.

"So you'll wait?" she asks hopefully, and I hate to cut that hope down but I have to. I owe Granny the truth. I will never lie to her. Plus, she'd beat my ass if I tried.

"No," I answer. "I have to go."

"I hate that I'm not there with you."

"Me too. But you'll be better than ever soon enough and we will go on all the capers," I promise her.

"I like the sound of that," she says, and I can hear how tired she is. "I miss the capers. Those are always a good time had by all."

"Me too," I agree. "Now, get some rest."

"Please, Shell—" she tries one more time, but I stop her.

"I'll be careful. I promise."

"I love you, Shelby," she says softly.

"I love you too, Granny."

And with that, I end the call and set my phone down on the kitchen counter. I slide my feet back into my sneakers and grab my keys from the table. I need to find answers and I need them now. I'm so distracted that I don't grab my purse from the table by the front door. I don't even hear the faint buzz of my phone as it rings on the kitchen counter.

Later, I'd wish I had taken the time to grab both.

I would also wish that I had heeded Granny's warning.

But you know what they say, "live and learn." Hopefully, I'll live to see the end of this one. Too bad I'm not so sure.

CHAPTER 20

LIGHTS OUT

"**S**hit, shit, shit!!!" I whisper harshly as I try and untie the ropes that bind my wrists together.

"Oh good," a voice I have come to hate says. "You're awake."

I've cheated death a lot in my life, usually on a family vacation when my dad and I were doing something stupid and slightly dangerous that my mom should have put a stop to well before we got off the ground.

Like when I was nine and he kept flipping the kayak in Cabo and tossing his only daughter—who never really learned to swim—in the Pacific Ocean, all while my mom watched from the beach. One would think she would have said, "Hey Jack, don't let Shelby drown." Or something but whatever.

Or when I was three and learned that people who grow up south of Michigan never really master a toboggan at Snow World at SeaWorld. My dad and I ran over two moms, three kids, and a SeaWorld employee before we were asked never to come back again. I still shudder every time I see a sled and my back twinges whenever it's really cold out. Fortunately, that doesn't happen often in Southern California.

I have been kidnapped, shot at, and who knows what else, but I have survived it all. I think somewhere along the way, I grew to think that I'm invincible. But that's Superman's jam, not mine apparently, because I don't think I can come back from this one.

And the thick rope around my neck really chafes.

After I hung up the phone with my granny, I grabbed my keys and raced out the door. I should really learn to stop doing stupid shit like that, but I digress.

I raced up the I-5 to James's Carlsbad home. I used to make this drive all the time. I could probably do it in my sleep. I pace each landmark: the outlet mall, the car dealership, the kayak marina that stinks so bad you always question if you shit your pants like mean old lady Ruth in yoga class when you drive past it in the summertime. Real talk. Is there anything worse than a hot shit stink?

I was so focused on getting to James's house that I never bothered to check for a tail. Why would someone be following little ole me anyways?

I also didn't do anything smart like park down the road from his house. No, I parked my bright white Jeep right in front of it in the driveway just like I always used to do in the old days when we were an item and I didn't know he was banging my bestie on the side.

I never seem to think straight when my emotions are running high. Something I should probably work on. Maybe there's a Master Class for that . . .

When James and I broke up, I never gave him the key to his house back. I kept it on my keyring as a reminder to never let a man get that close to me again, because they will always hurt you. In the end, they always let you down, or in Trent's case, knock you into an empty grave. *Oh, the memories!* How I wish I could go back to the day that Trent and I met at that funeral and tell him to pack sand when he asked me out after trying to take a peek up my skirt.

I let out a frustrated sigh, because I know that even knowing how ended, I would've still loved Trent with all of my heart, because I will never love like that again. It was a once in a lifetime love, and I am glad I experienced it, if only for a little while.

Or at least that's what I'm going to tell myself when it doesn't feel like my heart is going to bleed out in my chest. I'm sure after about a year or seven, and a tequila factory worth of the shit, I'll feel that way. For now, it just freaking hurts and I'm sad. I am really fucking sad.

I should have listened to the key. But I didn't, and now I've used it to break into the house of a dead man. A man whose murder I am being framed for, which is highly unfortunate, because I really despise a cavity search.

I pushed the key into the lock and thanked my lucky stars that James was too arrogant of an asshole to think about safety and changing the locks on his house every so often. He was so confident in himself and the fear he caused in those around him that he was never cautious. He never played it safe.

Apparently, I was too, because I definitely wasn't paying attention to my surroundings like a good girl. This became abundantly obvious when something heavy crashed into the back of my head and then it was lights out—and not even in a fun way, like Shawn Merriman's old end zone dance.

And that brings us to now.

My head is pounding.

My head is pounding, and I'm having a nightmare. There is something I can't quite remember though. I just can't put my finger on what it is. But I know, *I know*, there is something I need to remember.

I blink my eyes. My vision is fuzzy, which is weird, because I have perfect 20/20 vision. I have never needed glasses, so I'm not sure why I can't see.

I raise my hands to my face and rub my eyes to try to clear them, but when I do, I encounter a problem. My hands are bound together with rope.

"Shit, shit, shit!" I whisper harshly as I try to untie the ropes that bind my wrists together.

"Oh good," a voice I have come to hate says. "You're awake."

"Bella?" I ask. I mean, clearly, it's her and she's going to kill me. I feel so foolish, like I should have known all along that it was her. I should have seen the signs.

"Of course." She smiles like the cat who ate the canary. "Who else would it be?"

"That does seem to be the question of the hour," I say as I take stock of my situation.

I'm sitting on a barstool that's precariously balanced on top of a small table. There is a heavy noose tied around my neck that hangs from the exposed beams in the great room of James's house. My hands are bound in front of me.

"So you have it all figured out?" she asks.

"I don't actually," I answer honestly. Usually, I would try to keep the killer talking until someone could get here to help me, but there's no one. Everyone who would ride in and save me, who would back me up in a gunfight, has already turned their backs on me. I am absolutely all alone. That *really* sucks.

This is it. The end of the road.

Plus, one false move and I'm swinging like an old west bank robber at sun down.

"What don't you understand?" Bella asks.

"Why did you do it?" I ask stupidly.

"Isn't it obvious?" she prompts as she steps around the table to face me. "He wanted you."

"But I didn't want him," I reply a little more loudly than I meant to, and we both startle a bit. "I was with Trent. You could have kept James and left me alone."

"You stupid bitch," she spits. "I couldn't have 'kept James' as you so eloquently put it. He broke up with me and kicked me out. He decided he wanted you and only you."

"But I didn't want that," I say feeling the need to repeat myself. "I don't want that!"

"I don't care what you wanted or didn't want," she snarls, and I can see the crazy wheels spinning in her head. There's a weird light to her eyes that I have never seen before. It's like the lights are on but nobody's home, but it's not nobody, it's freaking Norman Bates! "But you don't care *what I want*. Sweet Shelby always gets what she wants."

"What are you talking about?" I snap, finally losing my grip on my composure. "He beat me!"

"He beat me too!" she yells back. "Only I stuck around, unlike you. I actually loved him."

"Why?" I can't help but ask. "Why would you stick around for him when he was a monster?" I can't wrap my head around it. James was a wolf in sheep's clothing. I had no idea the monster that he kept hidden deep down but once I got glimpse of it, I got the fuck out and stayed gone so I can't understand why she would have kept going back for more.

"Because I loved him! I have always loved him, and you got him," she explains and I feel like I just boarded a train for crazy town.

"I was dating him," I say, wondering if this chick—who I used to think of as my best friend—has ever cared about anyone in her life other than herself before now. "You met him, because he was my boyfriend."

"I am a victim of circumstance!" she shouts. "But you. Everyone falls in love with you, and I don't even understand why."

"Thank you?" It's an insult, I'm sure, but I'm about to die, so who the fuck cares? I'm not going to be polite here. She's a bitch and a fucking lunatic so I might as well go out with my head held high and my boots on. I mean, what do I have to lose anyways?

"I'm thinner than you. I'm prettier than you. Lord knows I'm better in bed than you. James used to complain that you were like fucking a dead fish. And yet he still wanted *you*!" She lists off and I'm wondering why James found me so fascinating if he thought all of those awful things about me. But I know the truth, it was Trent. If Trent hadn't been interested in me James never would have.

"He only wanted me because someone else did!" I shout back. "Can't you see that?"

"All I can see is that I am done losing to you. You can come in second now because it won't be me ever again."

"Don't you think I came in second when you were secretly fucking my fiancé all that time?" I snarl.

"Yeah," she agrees on a smile. "Wasn't it great?"

"Were you ever my friend at all?" I can't help but ask.

"Not really," Bella says as she shrugs. "You got invited to the better parties and I wanted to go."

"Wow," I say, feeling a little shocked. "Thanks."

"You're welcome," she preens on a sickly sweet smile. "Now, here's how this is going to go."

"I'm all ears," I say, trying for snark, but we can both hear the nervousness in my voice, because she smiles even wider.

"You are so distraught over killing James and then your life falling apart that you are going to hang yourself," Bella explains in a calm tone. "You've even been kind enough to leave a note."

"How are you going to play my bound hands and the table?" I ask.

"The table will be put back where it goes and your hands will be cut free. But you will swing just like you deserve," she says.

"Great."

"I know. Hey, you can thank me. We both know

this is better than prison," she says like she really believes that she's doing me a favor.

Between those two options, I'm not sure which I would choose, to be totally honest. Actually, that's a lie. I will always choose to live and to do it boldly as only I can.

"Now, let's get started," she chirps. "I have a coffee date with your boyfriend in thirty minutes to establish my alibi for this evening."

Wow, that hurts more than I thought it would.

"Is he in on it?" I ask. It would be just like her to steal another boyfriend of mine just for spite. The thought of Trent betraying me like that really stings.

"Wouldn't you like to know?" She smirks as she steps toward me. "Once I kick the table out from under you, it'll all be over."

"I'm going to have to stop you right there," comes a voice from the doorway. And when my eyes dart toward it, I see Trent, his gun trained on Bella. She and I were so wrapped up in our "who killed who" back-and-forth that we didn't notice the cops show up.

"You couldn't shoot me before I kick the table out," she challenges, and then she does just that. Her foot swings out so fast and so hard that the table is pushed out from underneath me in the blink of an eye. It's like watching everything happen in slow motion. I raise my hands up to try to grab onto the rope around my neck as the chair falls out from underneath me. I kick my feet wildly, trying to find purchase. The stool I was sitting on drops out from underneath me and I drop down and swing. Fuck! I'm really going to die.

"Shelby!" Trent shouts.

Pop! Pop! Pop!

I don't even flinch as gunshots sound in the room and Bella falls. I don't think it was Trent, because he started running toward me the second she kicked the table out from under me. He grabs me by my legs and lifts up to relieve the pressure on my neck but the lights are already dimming.

I remember in fourth grade when we learned about California history that there was a bank robber that was so tall and his feet dragged that it took over an hour to hang him. I kind of feel like that right now.

"I need some help here!" he shouts.

My fingers are numb where I've wedged them between my neck and the rope. The little black spots on the sides of my field of vision threaten to bleed over.

"A bus is in route!" someone calls out.

"Goddamn it!" Trent roars. "Help me get her down!"

"I love you," I whisper.

And then it's lights out. Again.

EPILOGUE

IT'S JUST THAT SIMPLE

The summer sun warms my face.

I'm lying on a lounger by the pool at Trent's house, which is exactly where I've been every day for a week. When I was released from the hospital, Trent loaded me up and brought me here.

Proclaiming I was "finally home where I damn well belong."

As it turns out, I wasn't alone after all. Trent and Kane knew right away that someone was trying to frame me for James's murder; they just didn't know who or why. But in order to stay attached to the case, they had to remain impartial. Jones, Daisy, and Alyssa were all working the case to clear me and catch the real killer. I was never in danger of going to jail, and I never lost any of my people.

Jones feels terrible. He has visited me no less than four times this week already, and he brought me flowers every day I was in the hospital. It got so bad that Trent started to joke that Jones was trying to steal me from him, until Daisy laughed and said she was better at giving blowjobs than me. Which is probably true, and she likes anal, which we all know I don't.

Get back, bald-headed giggle stick!

Anyway, he feels that if he were better at giving me the high sign to not go off the deep end, I wouldn't have almost died. As it turns out, they were not on a double date, even though it's clear the undercover cop—as I discovered his identity later—has the hots for Alyssa. They were working on my case. When Jones yelled at me, he was trying to wink. Who knew some people can't wink? And instead, he was just scowling. I didn't see it, because I was crying. They were going to give me time to cool down before telling me the truth in the morning, but I didn't wait that long to act on my hunch.

He really does need to work on his delivery, but I'm not going to tell him that. He feels bad enough as it is and he is such a nice guy. It would feel like kicking a puppy.

Daisy and Alyssa's P.I. business is still booming. Daisy and Jones are as hot and heavy as ever. And Alyssa isn't giving the undercover cop the time of day. We all have a standing bet as to how long it'll take him to wear her down.

Kane and I are fine and always were. He was not only helping Trent, but he and Sophia have some things in the works. I figure they'll tell us all their news soon enough but I think I know what it is and I'm so happy for them. But it's not my story to tell.

My mom and dad are home from their last international adventure. Mom swears the Swiss Guard are the hottest she's ever seen and have better bulges than the Royal Guard at Buckingham Palace. My dad is pretending like he doesn't hear us.

Granny is home from the hospital and raising hell. She's never been better, although she is mourning her breakup with trans fats and other high-cholesterol-inducing foods. I heard her tell my mom the other day that if she made one more tomato-based meal, Granny was going on a murderous spree. My dad wisely took us all out to a steakhouse that night, in which he claims is was to avoid undue bloodshed.

I feel the lounger dip down on one side as it takes additional weight just before strong, calloused hands massage my shoulders. I smile but I don't open my eyes.

"We have to be fast before my boyfriend gets home," I whisper, and a gentle slap rains down on my upper thigh, making me laugh.

"Excuse you," Trent says.

I open my eyes and stare into his handsome face. "I knew it was you all along."

"Sure you did." He pouts a little, but I can tell he's only teasing.

"Of course, I did," I say as I sit up and wrap my arms around him. "You're it for me."

"I know," he assures as he places a gentle kiss on my mouth. "You know I love you, right?"

"I do," I answer. I'm not sure where this blip of vulnerability I see in his face is coming from, so I tread lightly. "I also know I love you. Very much."

"Do you like being here?" he asks me. "In this

house? With me?"

"I do," I answer him slowly wondering where the third degree is coming from. I wonder if he's feeling guilty about what happened too.

"Good, baby."

Trent touches his mouth to mine one more time before taking my left hand in his. He plays with my fingers before pulling something from his jeans pocket and sliding it up my ring finger. That something is an antique engagement ring. The setting is made to look like a flower with the center holding a fairly large diamond. Smaller diamonds twinkle around the sides. I recognize it instantly, because I've seen Trent's grandmother, Marla, wear it off and on.

"Trent?" I whisper.

"She didn't want you to have anything less than the best, and I can't help but agree."

We sit there staring at each other. Trent links his fingers through mine before lifting my hand up to place a gentle kiss over the ring his grandfather gave his grandmother sixty years earlier.

"The way I see it, once we got out of our own heads, we were perfect for each other," he tells me softly. "No other woman ever truly fit into my life, because she wasn't you. You were made for me and me for you. It's just that simple."

"Trent—" I start feeling tears of happiness clog my throat.

"Marry me."

"Yes."

The second the word leaves my mouth, Trent crushes his lips to mine. I laugh and cry a little, but they're happy tears, because Trent and I are finally getting the life together that we have always wanted. We fall back to the pool lounger, Trent covering my body with his.

"I want you, but I don't want to hurt you," he admits. I won't let him ruin this moment for anything. This, right here, is ours and ours alone. No one else gets to interfere with this—not here, not today.

"You won't hurt me," I tell him as I raise my hands to touch the side of his face and bring his mouth back down to mine.

I arch my hips against his as I draw my hands down to his sides and slide them upward, pushing his T-shirt up as I go. Trent pulls away from me to reach behind him to pull his shirt over his head and drops it to the ground. I use the opportunity to grind my center against the front of his jeans, making him growl just a little bit in the back of his throat. The sound does things to me, really, really good things.

Trent grabs the waistband of my leggings and my panties all at once and rips them down my legs before throwing them to the ground. He runs a fingertip over my clit and down to slip inside me.

"Always so wet," he says.

"Yes," I whimper.

I try to rock against his hand, but he pulls away from where I need him the most. I don't have to wait long, because he unbuttons the front of his jeans and pushes them down his firm thighs as he covers me with his body again.

I feel the very tip of him at my center and then he slowly pushes deep inside. I cling to his shoulders and arch against him, rocking with him as he pumps deeper, hitting all the best spots.

I dig my heels into the backs of his legs to force him deeper and deeper as my body burns hotter and hotter. I'm so close. It won't take much to send me over the edge, and as Trent's movements become a little more erratic, I can tell he's close too.

And then with our arms wrapped tight around each other, we fall over the edge together.

"I guess we didn't need to rush it," he says to me as he plays with one of my curls while he holds me in his arms a while later.

"What do you mean?"

"I should have taken my time," he says, and I can hear the smile in his voice, even though I can't see it from where my head is resting on his chest. "It's not every day a man gets to make love to his fiancée for the first time. I feel sad that I didn't take my time with you."

"You don't like dirty fucks anymore now that you're going to be an old married man?" I tease.

"Oh, you know I do." He laughs as he grips my hip tight, pushing me against his hard length. "I plan on fucking my wife every chance I get. But I meant that I should have taken my time savoring the moment. Celebrate a little bit."

"We have all the time in the world," I tell him as I lean down to kiss him gently.

"We have forever," he promises as he rolls me to my back deepening our kiss.

"We'll go slower this time," I say as he crawls between my legs.

"I'm willing to try if you are." He chuckles.

"Why don't you give it your best go?"

And then he does. Eventually, we make it inside to a bed. Trent orders Chinese, and we eat it straight out of the cartons, sitting side by side, while I wear nothing but his grandmother's ring.

And later, much, much later, we call our families to tell them the good news. And I've never been happier.

Trent was right. We belong together.

It's just that simple.

SAN DIEGO METRO NEWS
Engagements and Weddings

*Staff Sergeant and Mrs. Whitmore of San Diego,
California are pleased to announce the engagement
of their daughter,
Shelby Lynn
to
Trenton Eric Foyle
of Newark, New Jersey.
Wedding details to follow.
Welcome to the shit show.*

THE END
(For Now)

PLAYLIST

Miss Me More—Kelsea Ballerini
Sweet but Psycho—Ava Max
Burnin' It Down—Jason Aldean
Blank Space—Taylor Swift
Jailhouse Rock—Elvis Presley
Back to December—Taylor Swift
Apologize—One Republic
Cop Car—Sam Hunt
Break Up in a Small Town—Sam Hunt
We Are Never Ever Getting Back Together—Taylor Swift
Love Me Harder—Ariana Grande & The Weeknd
Begin Again—Taylor Swift
What If—Kane Brown featuring Lauren Alaina
S-i-m-p-l-e—Florida Georgia Line

Turn the page for an excerpt of Attack Zone and Start Sophie and Kane's story.

attack ZONE Murder on Ice Mysteries

Feuds not Foreplay

"You have got to be kidding me," I growl as I see that big blond bastard climb from his truck.

The parking lot is dark still with the exception of the tall lights that pock the black asphalt. It's four in the morning so the sun won't be up for a few more hours. I should be the only one here. Something Kane and I had already argued out last night. I even won best two out of three on rock paper scissors.

"Better believe it, princess," he barks out as he pulls a gear bag from the bed of his truck.

"No. No no no no no. Put that back. You're not supposed to be here," I plead as I grab my own skate bag and toss it over my shoulder.

He sighs, "You know, you don't always have to be such a selfish bitch," I rear back as if he struck me. "You could share the ice."

"I'm here at four so I don't have to," I whisper.

He shakes his head as if he's trying to clear a bad

thought, erase something that didn't turn out right on an etch-a-sketch.

I look away. If ever there was anyone who could make me feel like a bug, like dog poop on your shoe, *less than,* it's Kane Fucking Green, and trust me, others have tried. I feel the burn in my nostrils. I refuse to let him see me cry. *Ever.* And Lord knows, I have cried my fair share of tears over Kane Fucking Green and I'm not going to shed another one. I'm just not.

I take a deep breath and turn on my heels and walk away from him. I feel his gaze burn my skin. It's not the only thing he's burned in the last year. He's burned almost every bridge I had. Literally, the only thing left in my life is figure skating. I feel him on my heels as I walk up the concrete steps at the front of my home rink, *Del Mar Ice House.*

The big glass doors and windows that line the entire front of the rink are dark. That's weird. Usually, Vadim turns the lights on when he comes in to unlock the doors for me. Maybe he's having a late start this morning. Although, that's not like him at all.

Most people think that my early mornings are crazy. That my four in the morning practices are insane. But I love it. I love the smell of fresh ice. I love the quiet time when I can pace through my routines free from distractions. It's my time to think or to not think, to clear my head and just be free. And my life is anything but free. Being a sitting Senator's daughter pretty much guarantees that, so I love this time to myself. I love mornings like this

Vadim, the rink owner, loves these mornings too. He's always here well before my early time slot. He unlocks the doors for me and turns on the lights. We once struck up a friendship over our love for Moscow. He was surprised to find out that I trained there for a whole summer under some of the best figure skating coaches in the world.

From that moment on, we were bonded. He's like a favorite uncle doting on his beloved niece. So Vadim took to surfacing the ice on the zamboni before I come in. Even though it was surfaced right before closing the night before. He sharpens my blades for me when I need it. And he's the best. No one can get me a better hollow. So it's surprising when the lights are still out upon my arrival.

Although he did double book this time with Kane as well. I was so mad when I found out Kane Fucking Green had weaseled his way into my favorite ice time. I need this time to clear my head. From people like *Kane Fucking Green*. I haven't been able to be in the same room as him since The Event.

Can you blame me? No, you can't. What he did hurt? He hurt me.

I look at my sterling silver *rolex* watch on my wrist. It's ten after four in the morning. That's so unlike Vadim. He should be here by now.

"What's wrong?" Kane asks, reading my mood.

"He's late," I say softly.

I reach for the handle of the door and it pulls free without effort. The door is unlocked. I pause for a second and then walk through the door. Vadim must be here after all. He must have forgotten to turn on the front lights.

"Wait, maybe I should check it out," he says as he

places his palm on my shoulder. I immediately stiffen.

I shrug off his hold. "You would just like that wouldn't you?" I growl. "Oh, sure, just go right ahead and enjoy my ice time while I stand here like an idiot in the parking lot, Kane." I roll my eyes.

"Is that what you really think of me, Princess?" he asks his voice low in warning.

"At this juncture, I'm not sure what to believe," I say honestly meeting his blue gaze.

"I suppose I deserve that," he sighs.

"I suppose you do. Now if you'll excuse me, I have a National Championship to prepare for," I say as I start walking down the hall towards the ice.

The rubber mats squeak under my sneakers. The shoes my Stepmonster hate with a passion, but they're so comfortable. Especially after a long workout on the ice. I head towards the team boxes. That's where I'll put on my skates and stash my music and my water by the boards.

Kane is beside me as we turn the corner and stop in our tracks.

Where the main building lights were off, the lights over the ice are on. The whir of the zamboni is deafening as it circles the ice top over and over. I gasp when Kane's hand closes tight over my bicep bringing me to a halt and I raise my head to see what he sees.

Vadim is sprawled back over the seat of the zamboni, his eyes point up at the championship banners of the local professional hockey team all lined up in a neat row — but they don't see them, they won't see anything again — the bullet hole between his blank eyes saw to that.

"Holy son of Scott Hamilton," I speak without thought.

"You got that right, babe. Whatever it is that that means," Kane says before he leads me back through the rink and out the glass front doors.

I open my mouth to say something, anything, but instead find myself racing over to the bushes to toss my cookies. Kane is behind me rubbing my back and making soothing noises. He hands me a water bottle from his gear bag before pulling his phone from his pocket.

"Dispatch, this is Detective Kane Green, badge number 57635. I need to report a homicide... " he says into his phone before lowering the volume of his voice. "And I have Senator Dubois' daughter with me."

Six months ago, I had hoped to put Kane Fucking Green and all of his bullshit behind me. I swore I wouldn't focus on anything but myself and this next Olympic cycle. Not my dad the U. S. Senator, or his bitch of a wife. And definitely not the feelings of hurt and betrayal that seeing Kane always seems to bring to the surface. Not to mention *other feelings*. My name is Sophia Eleanor Dubois, Sophie to my friends, and I have a funny feeling Kane Green just screwed me and my plans ... Again.

ABOUT JENNIFER

Jennifer is a thirty something lover of words, all words: the written, the spoken, the sung (*even poorly*), the sweet, the funny, and even the four letter variety. She is a native of San Diego, California where she grew up reading the Brownings and Rebecca with her mother and Clifford and the Dog who Glowed in the Dark with her dad, much to her mother's dismay.

Jennifer is a graduate of California State University San Marcos where she studied Criminology and Justice Studies. She is also a member of Alpha Xi Delta.

13 years ago, she was swept off her feet by her very own sailor. Today, they are happily married and the parents of a 10 year old and 8 year old twins. She lives in East Texas where she can often be found on the soccer fields, drawing with her children, or reading. Jennifer is convinced that if she puts her fitbit on one of the dogs, she might finally make her step goals.

She loves a great romance, an alpha hero, and lots and lots of laughter.

STALK ME . . .

www.JenniferRebeccaAuthor.com

ALSO BY JENNIFER

The Claire Goodnite Series
Tell Me a Story
Tuck Me in Tight
Say a Sweet Prayer
Kiss Me Goodnight

The Liam Goodnight Duet
Hush Little Baby, Coming 2020
Don't Say a Word, Coming 2020

The Funerals and Obituaries Series
I Met a Girl (A funerals Prequel), FREE on Wattpad
Dead and Buried
Dead and Gone
Dead and Deceived

The Murder on Ice Series
Attack Zone
Layback

The Southern Heartbeats
Stand
Whiskey Lullabye

www.jenniferrebeccaauthor.com/books

ACKNOWLEDGEMENTS

Thank you so much for picking up this copy of DEAD AND DECEIVED! I hope you have been enjoying Trent and Shelby's story as much as I have. I couldn't get to do what it is that I love without the readers and bloggers so thank you!

Thank you to Tricia Crouch for taking me on and keeping me sorted. I am so blessed to work with her! She takes such a weight off of my shoulders and makes it so that I can get back to doing what I love best, writing.

Thank you, thank you, thank you to Kayla for helping me out when I was in a bind, but also because she worked her ass off and made me look so good. She thinks I'm funny and I'm probably not. She understands that I work best in a little chaos and can laugh when I accidentally type "Fisting" when I meant something else. She's fantastic and I'm keeping her forever.

Thank you to Kruse Images and Photography for another wonderful cover image and to BT Urruela for continuing to be the face of Trent. As always, it's lovely to work with you.

Thank you to my sister from another Mister, Alyssa Garcia of Uplifting Designs and Marketing and all the other things. She is so fantastically talented. I babble a little about what I want and she makes magic. But also, she's my ride or die, my business partner, my platonic sister wife and I couldn't do it without her. I'm so thankful that I don't have to.

Thank you to Stacy Garcia of Graphics by Stacy for making me look so good. She is so talented and makes everything so easy. She's been my friend since she broke my toe in Austin and I am so very thankful for her in my life.

Last as always, but never least, thank you to my husband, Sean, for always believing in me. From the first moment I said "I have this crazy idea" he was onboard and never looked back. My big bearded sailor has made all of my dreams come true and loves telling people he has fifteen books written about his sexual prowess. He always makes me laugh and has never made me cry in thirteen years. He's the guy that sets the standard and I am so thankful that our son is learning from him what it means to be a man and our daughters are learning what it looks like to be treated with love and respect. Through all of life's ups and downs, I have never regretted a moment with him and I never will. I love you so much, Sean. It was only ever you.